The

Connect's

Wife 6

NAKO

LENEKO

129115

Acknowledgements

As I wrote the notes for *Connect's Wife 6*, I shook my head and laughed. I couldn't believe I'm writing yet another Connect's Wife book. This story was supposed to end three books ago, but somehow the readers and God felt otherwise. Thank you to every reader who supported my first series, to every positive and negative review, thank you so much. It has strengthened me as a writer and for that, I am grateful.

I found myself in Farren Knight, I never thought a character that I created in my downtime would have such a strong impact on my life and how I interacted with people, and even myself. Throughout this series, I have gone through a multitude of emotions. I'm sure it was pretty obvious considering parts two and five (LOL). I have lost close friends, a lover, and even people who I thought were family; however, I'm thankful for every situation that I have encountered. Every situation I found myself in were all lessons learned.

I would like to thank #ROBERSON5 for all of the love and support, late night food, and coffee runs and encouraging me when I wanted to give up so many times. I would like to extend my love to my family and friends, thank you so much for purchasing every book, promoting via word of mouth, and on social media.

I would like to thank my publisher, editor, and #TBRS for all of the love, support, and encouragement. I'm forever grateful, whether it's words of encouragement, quick girl talk, or a late night word count challenge, y'all have made me feel really welcomed into the family, and I am forever thankful.

And OMG!!!!!! All my hugs and kisses go to the SWP group on Facebook. I feel like I've met long-lost girlfriends, and the one thing we all have in common is, we WRITE! I love chatting with you all. I'm learning so much about black women and empowerment. Before joining the group, I was very uptight and secretive with how I operated due to past hurt in friendships. I soon realized that not everyone is out to hurt you. Thank you for softening my heart. Love y'all xoxo

I would like to extend love to my readers, everyone who reads my work, discusses it on social media and in their book clubs! I love when y'all hop in my inbox with questions and "what's going on" with the characters. I enjoy every conversation, I wish I could add all of you but that would be picking favorites LOL! I I'm thankful for my test readers who have no problem hurting my feelings when the book is moving slow or getting boring. Tonya Renae, Aliah Green, Keyshia, and my little sister, Narie Roberson, no book gets published if I don't have the green light from the Fantastic 4. Thank you for everything.

I pray that part 6 gives every reader the closure they were looking for in part 5. Thank you for the continued support and again this is really just the beginning. All things are possible through Jesus Christ.

With Love, NAKO

Introduction

Woman

noun wom·an \\'wu̇-mən, especially Southern 'wō- or 'wə-

According to Merriam-Webster's Dictionary, a woman is defined as an adult female human being, a woman who has a specified job or position, all women thought of as a group. That's a pretty cool definition, but if only Farren Knight was in the dictionary. Farren Knight, located right under the 'F' category. Farren Knight...an educated African-American woman, made it out of the slums, climbed out of poverty, fought her way through the struggle. Despite every setback, tragedy, loss of so many loved ones, downfalls and heartaches, Farren Knight remains a WOMAN. She remains you, she remains me, she resembles and reflects, a black woman. A black woman who takes care of home, mothers the children, cooks and cleans as if she's getting paid to do so, prances around in heels because that's what her man liked. Farren Knight is a WOMAN. A woman we all strive to one day be, a woman who didn't let life get to her; depress her...well not for too long. But she stayed strong. Her wrongs became her pillars of strength. Her hurt was turned into therapy. She allowed the bullshit she went through to mold her, to make her better. Farren Knight was that woman, and damn I hate to say this, so excuse my French, but it made her that BITCH, a bad bitch at that. Who do you know that was touching Farren Knight? None could compare. Even as Christian Knight took his last breath or laid in his cell at night, even as Dice cuddled with his wife and played with his children, even as Kool hopped down the hallways of that hotel that night he was supposedly murdered; as Mario came to her rescue on that summer day, as Jonte stayed by her side even though he didn't deserve her, they all loved them some Farren Knight. She was an amazing woman; she was the epitome of a black queen. Farren was the love of so many powerful men's lives. She was the air they breathed, the weed they smoked, the Bourbon they sipped, the holster to their .44, she was what they all needed to live...then die. Farren Knight captured the attention of every single person who she came into contact with. Even on her worst day, you would still never know, she was always too afraid to show it. She didn't believe in displaying weaknesses, she didn't believe in showing off her insecurities. When you saw her, you knew she was Farren Knight, without no second guessing. Farren Knight was one of a kind, men cherished her, hoes respected her; the original Connect's Wife, no matter how many wives came after her through The Cartel. They could all try their hardest, but none would ever compare to Farren Knight, the original heir.

On behalf of David Weaver Presents,

I present to you The Connect's Wife 6

Must read The Chanel Cavette Story: From the Boardroom to the Block, now available on Amazon Kindle Unlimited or for .99 to fully understand The Connect's Wife 6

Chapter 1

Farren Knight

The taxi cab driver called Farren and spoke in his native language. She responded calmly and hung the phone up. "What did he say?" the man in the room asked her.

"That he isn't being followed anymore and he's headed here," she said.

"Is he sure?"

"He said it was his word, so I trust him." Farren shrugged her shoulders.

"Are you nervous?" he questioned.

She looked over at him. He was cool and all, don't get her wrong, but he was overbearing. Farren had been taking care of herself since she was a child. She wasn't used to having someone cater to her every want and need, and she was extremely agitated and annoyed.

"No, should I be?" she questioned.

"I don't know, I never had a long lost sister," he told her, jokingly.

Farren walked out of the room and went to her bedroom. She spent her free time watching home videos and flipping through old photo books. She was missing her children terribly and she was unsure of how long she was going to be able to fake her death. Farren was a mother first before anything, and not being able to wake up and take care of her children was starting to affect her.

The day that she was "supposedly killed" was fucking crazy. After Greg killed Mari's ass and told her all of those revelations, she just knew that it was all over for her. Her mind went to her children and she prayed like hell they didn't suffer through life because of her and Christian's foolish decisions. Farren was worried that Noel and Morgan would look for love in the wrong places because of the lack of love and attention they didn't even get a chance to receive, because the two most important men in their life had both been taken away from them at a young age. Farren prayed for her children's well-being; all of this could have been prevented if she would have told her father "NO" way back when. Farren was always putting others before herself, always lending a helping hand and giving her last, but damn, who gave their last to her? Who looked out for her?

Farren was bleeding out on her own steps, and she thought to herself, *Where is my help, where is my rescue, how am I supposedly a member of The Cartel and I'm here by myself? Why don't have I security or protection?* Deep down she wondered was all this shit planned out.

Her eyes started to close and she could feel her heartbeat decreasing.

She still had nightmares of that night. Farren told herself months ago that God must have plans for her that she was unaware of because there was no way in hell she survived all of those bullets. The only thing she was sure of was that she couldn't wait to do, was climb on top of Greg's lap and seal his lips with a kiss of death. She planned on making his ass die a very slow and painful death. Farren created so many different ways she wanted to kill him; she just prayed that when the time came everything happened how she always imagined it to be.

"She's out there on the phone," her friend came and told her.

Farren ran out of her bedroom so fast. This dumb ass bitch. Did she not know who she was, or better yet, who Farren was? Or was she really clueless about who she was coming to see? Farren opened the door and the girl didn't even hear her coming, strike two.

She snatched the phone out of her hand and stepped on it. Farren wore heels every day, after being in a wheelchair for months and only praying that she would be able to walk or even function as she used to again, she didn't take anything for granted. Feeding herself, taking showers, wearing six and seven-inch heels, life meant everything to her right now and the only thing missing was her children.

The girl turned around and Farren was able to really get a good look at her; damn they looked just alike. Farren had seen her somewhere, she just couldn't remember. Sometimes her memory was a little fuzzy.

"Come on," she told her after the girl confirmed who she was. She walked slowly behind her sister into the house.

"Do you want lunch?" Farren asked her.

"Ummm yeah, well no. Yeah, I'm kinda hungry," she said.

"Yes or no?" Farren asked again. Chanel looked at her, wanting to go off, but she didn't. She told her yes.

Farren called off orders in Arabic to the chef and went in the opposite direction; she opened the French doors into a sitting room. She loved this house and often thought about having her kids sent to her and they just live happily ever after in this 2.3 million dollar estate, equipped with a full staff. Farren never left, she had no reason to, the house had everything she needed. All she did was write and pray. Farren had endured a lot in her life, almost too much. She kept asking God what was he trying to teach her. She wanted to learn and grow in every situation that she kept finding herself in. Farren wasn't like other women, she had put two and two together while she was recovering after the multiple surgeries she had. She knew that she had the ability to change the world, but until she figured a lot of shit out about The Cartel, she was refusing to return to the United States or even have contact with anyone. Everyone was suspect if you ask her, including her mother.

Chanel stared at Farren and there were so many similarities, but Farren had power, she walked like the world owed her something. Chanel didn't want to judge her before they even got the chance to converse, so she erased those thoughts and sparked up a conversation.

"This house is beautiful," she said.

Farren sipped her tea, "Who were you calling, your grandmother?"

Chanel's eyes got big, how did she know Big Mama?

"Yeah I was, just letting her know I made it safe, I'm sure she's worried now," she stated.

"Do you even know who you are?" Farren asked, crossing her legs.

"Uh, yeah I do, I'm Chanel Cavett, I own a business and I'm a single mother. I have been through shit, okay. I might not be who you are, but I'm damn sure not some dumb ass girl. Did you bring me here to make me feel like I'm beneath you?" Chanel snapped.

Farren remained stone faced. Chanel thought to herself, *this is one cold-hearted bitch,* but what she was not about to deal with, was disrespect. Farren didn't even greet her with a hug or a kiss, or it's a pleasure to meet you, nothing.

"I used to be just like you, wearing my emotions on my sleeve; feeling like somebody owed me something. Then... something happened. Oh yeah, I remember, everybody kept dying. I couldn't keep anybody close to me for a long time without them leaving me."

Chanel was confused. Why was she talking in riddles? This hoe was crazy and she was ready to go.

"I asked you who you were because it's obvious you don't know, if you did, you would think before you made some of the decisions you make. For instance, let's go back to the day I supposedly died. You went to James' apartment and threw up. Why would you not clean up your throw up? Now, what if the police came and took your vomit in and came to your house, took you from your daughter, Madison that's her name right, and charged you for your murder? Secondly, you didn't get your number changed after leaving my funeral. Why would you keep the same number that's stupid? Then oh, my all-time favorite, you came to my house without a gun. Girl, do you know I could have killed you? The cab driver who works for me, too, could have raped you. You spent the entire ride on the phone with your grandmother. News flash baby, Big Mama can't save you from the wrath of The Cartel! So again I ask you, do you even know who you are?" Farren asked.

Chanel sat in her seat, shaking, tears running down her face. Who in the fuck was this lady? Her perfect dreams about her sister, the lady she read about on the internet donating money to non-profit organizations around the city, was not the lady sitting before her. She had yet to crack a smile.

"I want to go home," she said quietly.

Farren said, "Okay bye."

Chanel stayed in her seat.

Farren looked at her, "I thought you were leaving honey."

"You're just like your mother," Chanel shot. She couldn't let this bitch talk to her any kind of way. Chanel was no pussy, she just didn't want to piss her big sister off too much and then she killed her ass.

Farren laughed, she laughed for so long, Chanel really thought she was psychotic or on a pill.

"Please don't tell me my mama scared you? Girl please, my mama ain't gone bust a grape," she joked.

Chanel didn't say anything. Farren continued. "Why did you come to my funeral?" she asked.

"You seem to know everything, hell, you tell me," Chanel spat.

"It's a lot of stuff that's sketchy, hence the reason you're in my home."

"Just wanted to see if you were dead for real, I wanted to meet you."

"But why?"

"Because I did okay. I don't have the answer you're looking for."

"So it's not because your nigga wants to join the cartel?" she asked.

Chanel's eyes got big. Damn, she knows Quincy too. "I know everything even what you think I don't know, I know it," Farren confirmed her thoughts.

"It wasn't about him. It was about me, I swear."

"Okay, so I'm here now, now what?" Farren asked.

"You're not who I thought you were going to be," Chanel told her, honestly.

"And what were you expecting?" Farren asked surprised.

The kitchen staff came in and brought trays of food. Chanel dived in, as Farren watched her eat They looked just alike, but they were two different people. She hadn't really figured her out yet, but she planned on it real soon. Farren needed her, but she wouldn't tell her that just yet. She had to make sure this girl, her sister Chanel Cavett, had the potential, and most importantly, the heart to handle something for her. If not, then Farren Knight might have to return to the states and come out of the dark on a few motherfuckers.

"Not this...not this evil woman. You don't even smile," Chanel told her with a mouth full of food.

"Let me tell you something, I lost my first boyfriend at nineteen and I was pregnant when he died, oh let me mention that I saw his best friend shoot his ass up in front of me, held his hand until he took his last breath. Fast forward about twenty years, my perfect life is disrupted, my husband leaves me for a fucking stripper, daughter dies, then my husband is killed and I find his body. Finally find love again, only for his ass to die too, then I find love again, well kinda, I still don't know what we had but he dies, and I forgot to mention my best friend dies, her boyfriend kills his self a few days later, I haven't seen my kids in almost fourteen months so for real, don't tell me you haven't seen me not smile, you don't know what the fuck I've been through. I have nothing to smile about," she told her matter-of-factly.

"What about your dad?" Chanel asked.

"Huh?" Farren asked.

"Your dad, our dad. He died right? You didn't mention him."

Farren rolled her eyes, "Have you ever met him?" she asked. From her research, she knew that she didn't, but Farren just wanted to be sure.

"Never," Chanel said sadly. She never knew how much her father missing from her life affected her until now.

"Well, he was okay don't get me wrong. I'm grateful for him, but he was one of those people that you love just because. You didn't miss out on anything, trust me," she said.

"How can you say that?' Chanel asked.

"Easy, I raised my damn myself. He sent money when I asked, other than that I rarely saw him besides the summer time and he was never there then," Farren told her.

"At least you had money."

"That my mama took," Farren laughed. It was easy for her to laugh about old times because Lord knows wasn't nothing funny back in the day.

"Are you the only child?" Chanel asked.

"I have a sister, Nikita, we call her Neeki, she lives in Texas," Farren told her. Chanel wanted to be her only sister... she couldn't explain why.

"You're not hungry?" Chanel asked.

"I don't eat meat anymore."

"Why?"

"I'm training," Farren told her quickly.

"For what?" Chanel questioned.

"To kill someone," Farren told her seriously.

Chanel's heart stopped, this bitch was crazy.

"Are you for real?"

Farren nodded her head, her friend peeped his head in the room.

"Everything okay?" he asked.

Farren said, "Yes, we're catching up. Come in," she told him.

Farren's heart softened around him, and Chanel peeped it.

"Chanel, this is my friend Mario, Mario, my lil' sister Chanel," she introduced the two.

Mario said hello, and whispered in Farren's ear, "Shipment is here."

She nodded but didn't offer a verbal response.

Mario smiled at Chanel once more before walking out of the room and closed the doors behind him.

"That's your boyfriend?"

"Girl hell nah!" she said.

Chanel laughed. Farren was hood, don't get it twisted, but she had some swag about her, like a modern day Jackie-O or Grace Kelly.

"He likes you," Chanel noticed.

"Too much, he's cool though it's just not there. I keep trying to make myself like him, it's not happening," she admitted. Farren enjoyed talking to her sister. She had been confined to the walls of this house for months. The only people she had conversation with, was when she was yelling at the television when she was watching *Game of Thrones* and her favorite daytime show, *Wendy Wliilliams*.

"Why though?" Chanel asked.

Farren took a deep breath, she was done with love, it had failed her too many times. At night, when she laid in bed crying because she missed her children, she prayed for Dice, Christian, Jonte and Kool's souls. She had poisoned all of these men, and because of her, they were no longer here. Farren refused to sink her claws into another man, but then again how could she? She was considered dead; she had no identity, nothing.

"I'm not the one to love," she said, solemnly.

"I feel the same way, but I still have faith that I'm going to find love, get married, have more kids and travel the world," she said.

"See, I've done all that. My husband was the best husband in the world before he started cheating. He set the bar high for other niggas."

"Do you miss him?"

"Girl, more than you or anybody else could imagine. There weren't men like Christian Knight walking around Hardy Projects. I lucked up when I met him," she said.

"Oh my God, I went there looking for your mom, those people was like the damn secret service," she said.

Farren burst out laughing. "You went to Hardy by yourself?"

"Yes, like an idiot! I was so fucking scared."

"I'm surprised they didn't take your ass down through there."

"One lady, she looked like a crackhead, she threatened me to get the fuck on."

"Hardy don't play honey."

"You weren't scared growing up over there?" Chanel asked.

"Girl, I love me some Hardy. My mama used to have to come outside and get me!" Farren told her.

"That's the real projects, you don't even look like you from Hardy," she said.

"That's cus I spent the summers in California, and my stepmother was white," Farren said honestly.

"So your dad, our dad, was married to someone else after he left your mom?" she asked.

Farren looked up at her, "You really don't know anything do you?"

Chanel shook her head.

Farren sat back and stared at her.

"I need to talk to my mom first," Farren said.

"Why?" Chanel asked.

"Cus hell, I'm confused too," Farren stated.

"Your mother is mad rude yo," Chanel said.

"She has always been that way. I don't know her to be no other way," Farren laughed.

"That doesn't bother you, that she's not warm and fuzzy or loving?"

"Was your mother warm and fuzzy?" Farren shot back.

"Never met her, I wouldn't know," Chanel snapped.

"I'm from the hood, we're taught to survive and make it out of the hood by any means necessary. My mama never sugarcoated anything with me or my sister, I'm thankful that she didn't actually. I didn't grow up with fairytale dreams; my mama didn't tuck us in at night, none of that shit. We raised ourselves," Farren said.

Chanel just remained quiet. It seemed as if no matter what she said, Farren had an attitude or a harsh response, so she just felt it best not to even say anything.

"How long are you here for?" Farren asked, finally nibbling on a piece of fruit.

"Prob tomorrow morning or so, not sure yet," Chanel told her.

"Is there something you wanna say?" Farren asked. She had learned a long time ago how to pick up on facial expressions, moods, spirits, and everything.

"No, there isn't," Chanel told her, matter-of-factly. She couldn't stop staring at her older sister, she was strikingly beautiful.

"I have to go train, let me show you to your room." Farren stood.

"Do you miss your kids?" Chanel blurted out.

"Of course I do, we will be reunited soon, really soon...I just have to cross one motherfucker out." The glow left Farren's eyes when she made that one statement.

Farren couldn't understand how Greg really thought he was going to live happily ever after. Every single night before she closed her eyes to rest, he crossed her mind. He invaded her nightmares, because gone were the days where Farren went to bed dreaming about happy things. Farren couldn't sleep good at night knowing his ass was roaming around the city, enjoying life and making plays, and more than anything, making money that he had no right to make. Greg came up the wrong way; he crossed everybody out that looked like they could be a threat. Greg didn't get anything the honest way, he didn't know how he was manipulative, conniving, and in the words of Christian Knight, a "pussy ass nigga" and a pussy ass nigga didn't deserve to live at all.

Farren couldn't eat or breathe properly without wanting to kill him, but she knew that she had to handle him properly. She couldn't half-step the job or it would cost her big time. Farren knew good and damn well she was not a cat, she knew that she couldn't escape death too many times. When you belonged to The Cartel, bullets had names on them, so she had to be extremely careful, which is why she had been ducked off in Dubai for the past year. She prayed that her children were safe and sound.

Chloe was a damn good mother to her own children, so she knew they were being treated well, but nobody could raise her kids like Farren could.

Farren knew that the time was coming for her to hit the streets and handle her business, she just had to do everything the right way. Chanel came snooping around at the right time. Farren needed her and she had to train her in the way that she had been trained. Farren loved The Cartel, she wouldn't deny that, but people change and shit happens. She wasn't feeling the secrets, the lies, or the betrayal. She had to get from 'round them conniving ass niggas and raise her kids. They had nobody but her at this point. Christian Knight had been murdered and so had Jonte. Farren was giving it all up, but that didn't mean Chanel couldn't step up and handle business.

"I'm kind of tired, no lie," Chanel said, yawning.

"Get some rest, dinner will be prepared when you wake," Farren told her, after showing her to the guest suite.

Farren went into her room and changed into all black. Mario snuck up on her, she hated when he did that shit. She was already paranoid and popping pills left and right to stay relaxed.

"Don't do that," she hissed.

He threw his hands up in surrender, "My apologies, just coming to check on you," he said so kindly.

Farren took a deep breath. She didn't want to be rude, she just had a lot going on and on top of all of that, she was missing her kids and was tired of being in this house.

"How was it?" he asked, leaning on the bathroom counter, watching Farren closely as she undressed. Despite being in a coma, and going through multiple surgeries to restore her organs, she was still one of the baddest bitches he had ever been in contact with.

"She was actually cool, not as dumb as I thought she was going to be honestly," Farren said.

Mario laughed, "Y'all look like twins."

Farren looked at him, "You think so?"

"Yeah, just alike. I told you, at your funeral Noel thought she was you," Mario told her.

"I miss my baby," Farren said sadly.

"In due time," Mario told her, grazing her arm, before leaving the room. Farren had to get her mind ready for war; she placed thoughts and memories of her loving family to the back of her head, and cracked her neck as she slid into her Timberland boots. Farren jogged in place, in an attempt to increase her heartbeat. She loved training, she loved practice, this is when nothing else mattered but BLOOD, pure fucking red blood. She had to kill Greg, she really had to. There would be no peace without it. Farren loved the city too much. She loved going out to eat, getting her nails done, shopping, and going to the movies. All of that had come to an end once she realized she was still breathing. She couldn't believe that she was still alive....

Farren refused to pay a man thousands of dollars to train her, then it was a risk that they would be working for The Cartel, so she trained herself. She bought books on the art of karate and all kinds of other crazy terrorist shit. Farren had learned how to make bombs and how to kill someone in their sleep without leaving any bruises or signs. She learned how to pick locks and shut down alarm systems. She was turning herself into a modern day crook, but it all served a purpose. Before killing Greg, she planned on making his life so fucking miserable it would be ridiculous. Four hours later, two hundred and forty minutes to be exact, after Farren's body was over exerted and she could barely walk back to the house from training in the field, Farren slid out of the bear claw bathtub full of Epsom salt and lavender body oil. She dressed in leggings and a t-shirt and went to wake her sister.

Chanel was snoring lightly. Farren tapped her twice; she didn't budge, so she pulled her big toe hard as hell.

Chanel popped up quickly. Farren told her in a very serious tone "You need to get a gun, what if I came in here to kill you?" she said and headed for the door.

"Dinner is ready, take the elevator to the fourth floor," she said and closed the bedroom door. Farren clenched her cell phone in her hand, wanting to call Chloe's cell phone to speak to her kids, but the guard that Mario had posted outside of her house had already told Mario that the kids were already in the bed.

Farren picked around her plate. She really wanted some barbecued ribs, baked beans with cheese and ground beef, her mama's potato salad because she always puts a lot of eggs in it, a hot dog with a toasted bun, and a big cup of grape Kool-Aid.

"You weren't hungry?" Mario asked.

"This not what I had a taste for," she said, quietly.

Chanel was tearing her food up, "It's good to me," she said.

"I think I'm going to cook tomorrow, I can't take it anymore," Farren said.

"You can cook?" Chanel asked, surprised

"Girl yes, throw down. I used to cook three times a day, my husband ain't play that." Farren wagged her finger.

"My big mama cooks a lot, I can't cook shit but noodles and eggs," she said.

"Oh no, we gotta work on that, you gotta get you a husband and that ain't the way to get him sweetheart," Farren schooled her.

"I'm with that!" Chanel said cheerfully.

Farren smiled at her and Mario did too.

"I have to leave now, nice meeting you again," Mario stood and told Chanel. Farren knew he wanted a goodbye kiss, but she just wasn't in the mood for any of that. Mario waited around for Farren to stand up. She looked at him and he looked back at her. Farren threw her towel on the dining room table, "Excuse me, Chanel, I will be right back," she told her sister and followed Mario to the back door.

Even though he had been waiting hand and foot on Farren, he still had a business to run in Miami, so every few days he was flying back and forth. Farren was grateful for him, she really was, but it just wasn't there. Mario held her hand as they walked through the hallways. "I'm going to miss you," Mario told Farren.

"You'll be back soon," she told him. Farren looked forward to Mario leaving every week, and couldn't wait 'til his ass dipped. Even though it was bad, Farren was praying that something tragic happened in Miami so he would be forced to stay there for longer than four days. She needed time to think and map out her next move, and she wasn't able to do that with him under her every day all day. Farren had to lock her door at night because he was always coming up with some stupid excuse to come in her bedroom, and then fall asleep.

Farren kissed his cheek once they made it to the door where the car was waiting to take him to the airport. Although he was flying on a private jet, he still had to stop by the airport to make sure everything was together with a shipment. Mario handled his business well, and Farren had been learning a lot from him in the past few months. Mixed with the wisdom that Christian Knight had instilled in her, Farren Knight was starting to feel like she was on top of the world. If only she wasn't "dead" she could be killing the game right now. Farren had so many ideas she wanted to bring to The Cartel, but it was all good, she planned on living vicariously through her sister.

"FaceTime me tomorrow when you wake up," he told her, holding her tight. Farren smiled; he didn't see her roll her eyes because he was too busy in his phone.

"Okay boo," she told him in her sweetest tone. Farren stood in the doorway and waved happily until his car pulled off. She slammed the door and shouted "Hallelujah!" Farren was happy as hell; she crip-walked, moon danced, and did the Nae-Nae up and down the hallways.

"What are you doing?" Chanel asked as Farren's heart stopped.

"Shit you scared me," Farren told her.

"My bad, I was headed up to my room. I'm still sleepy," Chanel said yawning.

"Oh okay, I'm about to go watch movies. It's hard for me to sleep at night, well hell, even through the day," she mumbled. Farren refused for a bitch ass nigga to catch her slipping ever again. She had guns stowed all over this house.

"What are you going to watch?" Chanel asked.

"My wedding," Farren said sadly.

"Your wedding?" she asked again, Chanel was unsure if she heard her sister correctly.

"Yes, I used to watch it every night when my kids fell asleep, it was the best day of my life," Farren told her.

"Wow, that's weird."

"It's really not, come on you'll see," she told her, pulling her arm leading her to the movie theatre. Farren didn't have to do much, but cut the lights back off, grab her favorite throw and a bottle of water out of the mini fridge. Farren turned on a smaller television to the left of the big screen, which displayed all of the cameras positioned around the inside and the outside of the house. She sat Indian style on the floor and sat her gun in front of her.

Chanel was still in shock from earlier, this girl had guns everywhere. Farren pressed play on the remote control and began to watch her wedding from the beginning as if she had never seen it before. She wiped tears from her face after her and Christian Knight said their vows. Not only was her wedding super expensive, but it was so magical. Anything that she wanted, Christian Knight made it happen.

It was crazy because Farren remembered the day she woke up from a coma, to an army of guards surrounding her. It took a minute for her thoughts to register and her brain to reconnect to society. The feeding tube was so uncomfortable and she couldn't even swallow the gunk that was stuck in her throat. She started panicking and trying to pull the tubes out of her mouth.

One of the guards ran out of the door, and seconds later an Indian doctor and his staff came rushing in, "OH MY GOD, she is up!" one of the nurses screamed.

Another guard pointed his gun at her. The doctor threw his hands up to calm him. "She's just surprised, we have never seen someone survive so much damage," he said in awe. He couldn't believe she was alive. He just knew she would be a vegetable for the rest of her life, but the man who saved her life, clearly instructed him never to pull the cord, no matter how expensive it got. He had faith that she would come back... and damn if he was right. Farren Knight was breathing and on her own at that.

The doctors ran a few tests and checked her vitals, she was up, it was true. He asked her repeatedly, multiple questions.

"Sir, I hear you okay. For the twentieth time, my name is Farren Knight. I am okay. Please get me a phone?" she asked.

Mario entered the room, "I don't think that's best," he said.

Farren got scared, what the fuck was he doing there? Did he come to finish the job? Was this motherfucker working with Greg? Damn, she was doomed!

"Kill me now," she told him and closed her eyes.

Mario laughed, "I wouldn't have spent hundreds of thousands of dollars if I wanted to kill you, I would have just let you bleed out in your house," he said.

"And that's funny to you?" she asked, confused.

"Why did you close your eyes like you were prepared for death?" he asked.

"Where am I? Where are my kids?" Farren asked.

"Look, get some sleep, we will talk about everything when you wake up, I promise," he told her.

"No, I want to know where my children are," she told him.

"Look, you're dead so you can't go running after them right now, trust me."

"Huh? Nobody knows I'm alive? But why? So my kids think I'm dead!" she yelled.

He came over and placed his hand over her mouth, he bent down and whispered in her ear, "Shut the fuck up, and let me handle this for you. Just trust me," he told her quietly.

He stood back up and smoothed out his Valentino cotton t-shirt. Farren reached her hand out trying to grab his arm. She couldn't yell anymore; her body was weak, and her throat was hella sore.

Mario gave her his full attention, as he had been doing for months.

"My house...I need you to go get some stuff for me, please?" she asked.

"It's a crime scene investigation still, they're not giving up on finding your killer," he told her shaking his head.

Farren pleaded with her eyes, they were somehow full of hope. "Please...I need my wedding video and it's in a box in my closet, a Prada shoe box. Please, get it for me?" she asked.

Farren didn't care about shit else in that house, but that box had her life in it and that video was her therapy. That video captured her and Christian Knight's happiest memories; she had to have it.

"Okay, I'll try," he assured her.

"Please, it's in the basement," she whispered.

Chanel snapped Farren out of her thoughts. "Damn, how much y'all spent on this wedding?" she asked.

"Girl too much damn money, but hell, he had it, he didn't care," Farren told her sister, wiping her tears from her eyes.

"How did you really know he was the one for you?" Chanel asked.

"It felt right. We waited a good time before we took that step though. There were no secrets; we kept it so one hundred with each other. Every day when I woke up whether I was with him or not, he was on my mind...I can never describe how happy he made me," she said, honestly.

"I want to feel that one day," Chanel said, staring at Farren waltzing around at her reception.

"Whoa...go back...I know him!" Chanel said, standing.

Farren knew exactly who she was referring to, but she said nothing.

"Who girl?" she asked.

"Him! Why is he there? Do you know James?" Chanel asked.

Farren acted like she didn't. She got up close to the television, and stared at the paused screen for a few seconds.

"Nah, that's probably somebody Chrissy knew," she said.

Chanel stared at his face for a long time, and Farren peeped it.

"Let's get some rest. Tomorrow we're going to go into town because I'm going to cook. I gotta eat something familiar," Farren said, standing up. Her back was hurting and she needed to take her medicine and give her therapist a call, but she was trying to wean herself off those pills. She was too damn old to be picking new poisons, but those pills made her feel so good; better than sex, better than head, and better than some good ass weed, and Dubai had that good sticky.

"Farren, you were not going to come in my room and try to kill me were you?" Chanel shouted down the hallway.

Farren looked back at her and smiled, "Of course not, we're sisters, we're all we got," she winked.

Chanel didn't know if Farren meant what she just said, so she didn't offer a reply. She took the steps two at a time and returned to the room Farren told her was hers. The mattress felt like it was filled with clouds and feathers, she knew she was about to get a good night's rest. Farren was tired of sleeping alone; she missed kissing her kids goodnight and praying with them. She missed life in general. Farren knew that her time was coming to an end in Dubai, she felt it. Farren clenched her pillow tight, wishing it were Dice, reminiscing on the way Christian Knight used to hold her at night; closing her eyes smiling at how Jonte used to rub on her booty when they were watching the news, giggling at how laid back and smooth Kool was. Farren needed to get her mind together, she was confused and lost about so many different situations. But one thing was for sure... Greg was going to die. And on that note, sleep consumed her and she dozed off with a smile on her face.

Chapter 2

"I'm going home today," Chanel told her sister. They had just finished breakfast and were preparing to take a yoga class via YouTube in the theater. Chanel was really enjoying herself in another country, but the reality of the situation was that she had a child to get home to, a business, and most importantly a life. Farren didn't allow her to use any phones while she was in Dubai, but she did send a few emails out. Chanel had shit to handle. Although she was able to say she had finally met her big sister and established a relationship with her, she had to get back to Atlanta. The joy sunk from Farren's face, she loved being with her sister. They had so much in common and every night they stayed up swapping war stories and were learning about each other. Farren hated that so much time had been lost, but she knew that everything happened for a reason.

"Oh girl, I know you weren't going to stay forever," Farren said jokingly.

"I'm going to come back in a few weeks though," Chanel told her.

"No, no, I understand, trust me. You flying commercial or you want me to let the pilot know to gas up the plane?" Farren asked.

Chanel hated how quickly Farren's spirit would go cold; Farren ain't play no games, with the quickness she would shut her sister out.

Chanel told her, "It doesn't matter."

"I'll feel better if you flew back privately, make sure you get home safe and sound, anything can happen at the airport," Farren told her.

Chanel nodded.

"Well I'm going to let you pack and stuff. We can go to lunch before you leave," Farren told her, grabbing her yoga mat and towel leaving the room.

Farren's hands were shaking and she felt herself about to cry, but she didn't know why. Well she did, but she didn't want to admit that she didn't like being alone and that she really cherished her sister's company. Once she left, Farren would probably start back popping pills and thinking of suicide again. She didn't need that to happen, she needed to stay focused on the task at hand.

Farren paced back and forth in her closet. At a stressful time like this, she would call someone to help her make a big decision, but she couldn't. One, she couldn't use any cell phones, two, she had no one to call, everyone was fucking dead. Farren pounded her head on the wall, she couldn't think straight.

"Uh, what the hell are you doing?" Chanel asked.

Farren turned around, "Nothing, what's up?"

"Returning your jacket and other shit I borrowed." Chanel handed her a Tory Burch laundry bag full of items.

"Girl, keep that shit," Farren told her.

"Are you sure?" Chanel asked.

"Yeah," Farren told her.

Chanel said okay and left the room.

Farren damn near bit all of her nails off contemplating on whether she was staying in Dubai or going to handle Greg and get her life back. Mario was going to be pissed if he got back to the crib and she was gone. He had been telling her now was not the time for her to go fucking shit up, but Farren wanted to know when would the time be right, there never was a perfect time. She couldn't let any more time escape her, she was all her children had.

An hour or two later, Chanel came down the steps calling Farren's name. She had accumulated so much shit in the past two weeks it was ridiculous. All Farren did was shop and her new hobby was spoiling her little sister.

"Farren!" she yelled.

"I'm right here, here I come," she said. Chanel turned the corner, and saw her sister pulling a Fendi duffel bag down the hallway. Farren was dressed to the fashion gods; she was looking fly as hell. Chanel had only seen her in leggings and sport bras or all black, but standing before her was a woman fresh off the runway. Farren had on white Joe jeans, hot pink Giuseppe pants, and a white wife beater. She was so icy; her body was dripping in diamonds. Her hair was pressed out, but she had a pink turban wrapped around the front and oversized designer frames covered her face.

"Where are you going?' Chanel asked.

"I need to crash on your couch for a few days until I figure some shit out, you live in Atlanta right?" Farren asked.

Chanel nodded her head.

"Okay, okay, yeah, that's cool," Farren told her, stuffing hundred dollar bills in a MCM book bag.

"Shit, I forgot my weed, here I come!" Farren told her sister, running back up the steps.

Chanel didn't know how she ran in those six-inch heels, but she did it with no hassle.

She came back with two Ziploc bags full of marijuana. "Okay, we gotta go before Mario gets back, he was just running out to run errands, come on," she told her, throwing two of her bags over her shoulders. Chanel couldn't do anything but laugh, this girl was crazy.

The flight was smooth. While Chanel slept and snored, Farren made a to-do list on everything she needed to do in the next seven days. She was giving herself seven days to map shit out before moving in and killing her target. Farren knew her first stop was going to see her lying ass mama. Farren powered on another phone and one more after that one. She made sure her gun was fully loaded, and checked her face for the third time, before she told the pilot that he could open the door to the plane. They had been on the plane for an hour waiting on Farren to say she was ready to get off.

"Can I use your phone?" Chanel asked.

"Yeah, but who are you calling?" Farren asked.

"We gotta get a ride home, I'm about to call my assistant," Chanel told her sister matter-of-factly. Farren was now on her turf, she was now able to show her sister that she was a boss too.

Farren laughed, "Okay you can call your assistant when we get to Atlanta," she said, stepping down the steps.

"Where are we?" she asked.

"My neck of the woods, Jersey," Farren looked back and said with a big smile.

Chanel took a deep breath; she was ready to go home. Why didn't she just hop on a normal flight, like regular people? Chanel had so much to learn about The Cartel and her sister. Farren hadn't flown on a commercial flight in years.

"What we about to be doing?" Chanel asked.

Farren tipped some young boy a hundred-dollar bill to put her luggage in the trunk of a 2015 Escalade truck. Chanel didn't understand how she was making all of these moves with no identity, but she remained silent.

"You know how to roll?" Farren asked when they hopped on the highway.

"I don't smoke," Chanel said quickly.

"That's not what I asked you," Farren said.

Chanel smacked her lips. Farren's mouth was way worse than hers, but they were learning each other. Farren never meant any harm when she said things, it was the years of being a defense attorney that had her always sounding like she was prepared for war. Chanel split the cigarillo and got to work. She lit it and passed it to her sister. "Are you sure you don't wanna hit this?" Farren asked her.

Chanel shook her head. She had been clean for a few years and wanted to keep it that way. She hadn't revealed her dark dirty secrets yet to her sister, scared that she might judge her, but little did Chanel know, Farren already knew. Belonging to The Cartel, whether you're dead or alive, had its perks.

"You gone need it going to see my mama," Farren mumbled. She didn't pressure her sister to smoke, she didn't mind blowing the whole thing by herself. Farren parked the Escalade in a handicapped parking space once they made it to Hardy projects.

"Whoa...hold on wait, are you sure this is a good idea?" Chanel asked when Farren unlocked the doors.

Farren laughed, "This is my hood, we're good. But it's dark anyway, we're taking the back steps," she told her sister.

Chanel was still unsure. If Farren was attempting to lay low, she didn't feel like sliding through Hardy was a good decision and she was sure that if Mario was here, he would agree. Chanel stayed close by her sister, checking behind them every few seconds to make sure they weren't being followed. Farren was tired as hell, climbing all those steps to get to her mother's floor. She couldn't risk anyone seeing her on the elevator. Chanel laughed, "Girl you getting old."

Farren flipped her the middle finger.

"Knock on the door," she told her sister.

Chanel's eyes got big. "Me? Fuck no," she said.

Before Farren could tell her to grow up, the door opened and her mother said, "Girl I know your hips anywhere, bring ya ass in," she said and walked away from the front door.

Chanel looked at Farren, who couldn't do nothing but shake her head. Chanel whispered, "How did she know we was out here?"

"Girl she's fucking crazy," Farren told her, entering the home. Nakia, Farren's mother, was sitting on the couch, smoking a cigarette.

Farren fanned the smoke out of her face and went into the kitchen.

"You ain't cook?" she yelled from the kitchen.

"Girl no, cook for who? My kids grown," she said, never taking her eyes off Chanel Cavett.

"I see you found your sister," she said, smugly.

"Ma, leave that girl alone," Farren told her, reentering the living room.

Nakia ignored her daughter. "When you get here?" she asked.

Chanel wondered did her mother know she was alive this whole time, because she didn't cry, jump for joy, or anything.

"Just now, this was my first stop," she said.

"Hmmm, so who you been ducked off with?" her mother asked nosily.

"I need you to get the kids," she ignored her mother and ran off instructions.

"I'll try, but that crazy ass bitch fought me tooth and nail for custody of them kids. Neeki jumped on her after we left court," she told her daughter.

Farren never responded... her mind went elsewhere. She just wanted her kids; she didn't want to hear what all they had been through in her absence.

"Ma, did Daddy know about Chanel?" she asked.

Nakia blew more smoke out of her nose, and put her cigarette out.

"Yeah, but he was in denial, but hell, that wasn't new with your daddy," she said, dryly.

"So where is her mama?" she asked, as if Chanel wasn't even sitting there.

"Dead," Nakia said looking directly at Chanel. Farren peeped the tension and she wondered what was that about.

"But why?' Chanel asked.

"Because she was a sneaky ass hoe," Nakia said nonchalantly.

"Ma!" Farren yelled.

 Chanel shook her head and went to the window. Although she never had a chance to bond with her mother or have a conversation with her mother, she still wasn't with the disrespect.

"I'm serious, don't ask no questions you don't want the answer to," she said.

"What happened? The girl needs closure," Farren told her mother.

Nakia took a deep breath, "Whew I need a drink," she said.

Farren stood, "I got you, speak up so I can hear, sis you want a drink?" Farren asked.

Chanel nodded her head. Nakia rolled her eyes when Farren called her "sister". In Nakia's eyes, she was a bastard child. She hated Chanel Cavett just off the strength of her trifling ass mother.

"I met Colette...well Coco, at the corner store; lil' skinny thang she was. She was in there buying a pop or something, I can't remember..."

"Man Luis let me get a damn smoke, you know I'm good for it," a young and eager Colette yelled to the Arab behind the glass window in the local corner store.

"No, no Coco, that's it, you and your mother owe me plenty of dollars," he fussed.

Colette was trying to be nice to his lil' ass, but she had no problem stealing the shit and running off. She knew that he was in the store alone, which meant he couldn't run from behind the counter and risk one of the jack boys running up in the store and robbing him for everything in the cash register.

"I promise this the last time, my mama waiting on her food stamps to get here man," she lied.

"Coco get out of here," he fanned her away.

Colette went to ask him one more time but a deep and raspy voice came from behind her and said, "Put her shit on my tab." Coco turned around to tell the lady she ain't need no handouts.

"I'm good lady," she said rudely. The short and dark skinned lady told her, "No worries".

"Well thank you," she said and grabbed the single Newport and her pop and walked out of the store. As she crossed the street and started walking down the block, the same lady came up beside her in a red Mercedes-Benz.

"You need money?" she asked.

Colette knew this ugly ass lady wasn't no dyke. "You got the wrong one," Colette said shaking her head.

The lady let out a hearty laugh. "I have a few job openings down at my company if you're interested. No hard labor and it pays cash every Friday," she said.

Colette stopped in her footsteps, "Where bout?" she asked.

"Hardy Projects."

"Hardy? The hood? Oh hell nah, I don't fool around in Jersey, I'm good," she told her and kept walking.

"You're safe with me, ask about me. My name is Kia, you'll see me again," the lady said and peeled off down the street.

"So then what happened and Ma, when did you have a red Mercedes Benz?" Farren asked.

"Girl, a long, long, long time ago," she said.

"How long was it before you saw her again?" she asked.

"Girl, I ran into her at a poker party, you know I don't play about my gambling," she said.

Farren mumbled under her breath, "Tell me about it."

"I saw her at a poker game, she was a lil' tipsy but she knew what she was talking about. The girl was not a dummy I will say that. She told me she wanted to come make some money with me."

Chanel asked, "Money doing what?"

Nakia took a sip of her drink that her daughter had just handed her.

"Cook some dope for me," she said.

Farren choked on her alcohol. "Stop being dramatic," her mother fussed.

"For you? Huh? Ma, what are you talking about?" she asked.

"This was all a very time long ago."

"You had money?" Farren asked loudly.

"Farren shut the hell up talking all loud."

"No for real, you had money?" Farren asked again.

"I had a lot of money," Nakia said matter-of-factly.

"Shit where it's at, we struggled our whole damn life!" Farren said angrily.

"Your selfish ass father...your fucking father and that damn Bianchi," she said with so much bitterness and malice in her voice.

"What you mean?" Chanel asked.

Nakia got up and paced the floor. "Hold on," she said.

Nakia left the apartment and locked the door behind her.

"Where she going?" Chanel asked.

Farren ignored her. She knew her ma had another spot on this same floor, but that wasn't Chanel's business. No one was ever allowed into it and she didn't understand why, but then again she never asked any questions. Farren could only imagine how many secrets her mother had been holding in over the years.

Nakia reentered the tiny apartment and sat down with a safe in her lap. She stuck her little hands between her breasts and grabbed a key.

"Ma, ain't no way that key been in there this whole time."

Nakia laughed, "Hell no, I just didn't want to drop it on the way back over here."

Nakia opened the safe and pulled out a photo. She blew the dust off it before smiling at the picture; boy did she miss the good ole days.

Farren snatched the photo out of her mama's hands and stared at it closely. "Ma that's you?" she asked in awe. She had never seen her mother dressed up, let alone in all red with a floor-length mink coat and a cigar hanging out of her mouth.

"Those were the days," she said proudly.

"Who are these people behind you?" she asked.

"My workers," she said, pointing to a few people.

"That's your father, Bianchi...you know Kim? That's her daddy right there and I bet you don't know who that is right there," she said.

Farren couldn't believe they all looked so young and naïve. The only person who wasn't smiling in the picture was her mother.

"So ma, to be clear, what you telling me is you started all this shit?" she asked.

Nakia nodded, "In Hardy, all by myself, me and my brother, God rest his soul. Some hating ass niggas came in here and robbed us while I was out of town, killed my mama and lil' brother," she said sadly.

"Are you serious?" Farren asked. She was super surprised.

"Yeah and your daddy...girl your daddy played me. I met him and he fed me all this bullshit. Him and Bianchi came right on in and took over my empire and made it theirs. Your daddy's parents had a whole bunch of money so he stayed an attorney but that was only to build bridges with the law. Your father was smart, I'll give him that, but I made him wise and Bianchi made him stupid at the same damn time. He let him get in his ear and snatched every single thing I worked for right from up under my nose, I never saw it happening," she said, lighting another cigarette.

"Why didn't you take it back, why you even give him your connect?" Chanel asked.

Nakia looked at her and Chanel even hated she said anything. "It was so complicated back then. Bianchi's family had money, but they had no clout in the streets. People fucked with me because I was from the hood, I got money in the hood and I never moved, ever," she said.

"Farad kept saying his friend wanted to holler at me, and I knew it was fishy but I was in love, so I met with him anyway. They basically told me that they were taking over my territory and I would get thirty percent."

"Thirty percent? Oh hell nah," Farren said, shaking her head.

"I went to call your father and he never returned my calls. We had a lil' spot ducked off in the city, went there and all his shit was gone. I was pregnant and everything. About three years after you were born, he popped up at my house randomly needing advice. Bianchi was taking over and didn't treat him like an equal partner no more. I told him fuck off," she said.

"Did he leave?" Farren asked.

"Of course not. I went and got a room with him for a few days, you know how that goes. Anyways, he was in the shower and his wife called his phone, of course I answered and hell, me and Diane been beefing ever since," she said.

"So ma, don't get mad when I ask this because I'm over it now I promise I am, but you mean to tell me I suffered because of some shit between you and my daddy?" Farren asked hurt.

Nakia exhaled. "You'll never understand how complicated our relationship was," she said.

"That's bullshit," Farren said, wiping her eyes.

Chanel finally saw her sister cry. She didn't even think she had emotions.

"So how did my mom die?" Chanel asked. She didn't give a fuck how mean and evil Nakia looked at her, she had been trying to solve this mystery for years. Today she was getting the answers she needed.

"Fuckin' Farad, her husband Simon found out and she thought Farad was going to play captain save-a–hoe, but he acted like he didn't even fuck with her like that, but hey, Farad was good for that," Nakia said.

"So who killed her?" Chanel asked.

"Her husband, Farad definitely wasn't no killer."

"Who knows, you over here in the hood hiding out, and you a damn mob boss," Farren said sarcastically. She was very agitated and irritated.

"I never even got to know her."

"It's life, The Cartel wasn't nothing to play with, I told her that when I met her," she said.

"'Play with fire, get burnt. It happens boo," Farren said standing up.

Chanel didn't understand how they could be so heartless in relations to her mother's death, especially Farren.

"Is my condo still up?" Farren asked.

"Farren, how am I supposed to know?" her mother said.

"We about to dip," Farren told her mom.

"Where have you been?" she asked.

"I'm not telling you," Farren snapped.

"Well what is your plan?" she asked.

Farren took a deep breath. "Look ma, I don't know, okay, I really don't know yet," she said.

"You tell me that you climbed out of your casket and you don't know what the fuck you came here for? Okay, let me tell you this, Greg is running shit and all the families hate it. So whatever you gotta do, make him first on your list," she said.

"Why they won't kill his ass?" Chanel asked.

"It's a system, they do shit by the books," Farren tried to explain.

"System my ass, ain't no real niggas left," Nakia said, disappointed at how The Cartel has turned out.

"I gotta meet with James in a few days," Farren said.

Chanel's face lit up.

Nakia said, "Does he know, cus he thinks you dead?"

Farren laughed, "Don't let James wanna be James Bond ass trick you," she said.

Chanel couldn't wait to question Farren once they got in the car. She had heard her talk about James and admit that she loved him and they had a real connection. Farren sat up and listened to her talk about James as if she didn't know who he was at all. Chanel wasn't with the mental games at all.

"Wouldn't be James if he wasn't playing mind games," Nakia directed her statement to Chanel.

"I'll be in the car," Chanel said.

"Girl this is Hardy, wait on me, we about to go," she said.

Farren asked her mother did she need something, Nakia told her yes.

Farren peeled a couple of hundred dollar bills off and asked her mom, "So if you was the head bitch in charge, where all that money at?"

"Bianchi got in your daddy's head. It's okay though, it's all good," Nakia said. She had killed him and not once had she regretted her decision; he deserved to die. Bianchi was one selfish motherfucking bastard.

"I'll see you soon," she kissed her mother's cheek. Nakia was surprised at Farren's warm gesture; she had never been too affectionate with her mom, ever.

"Farren please be careful," her mom said. She knew her daughter could hold her own, hell, she had been holding it down this whole time.

"Farren?" her mother called out to her daughter one more time before they hit the stairway.

"Where were you?" she asked again.

"At one of Christian's houses," she said with a smile.

Farren got in the truck and locked the doors. She started the engine and reversed out of the parking lot.

"You hungry?" Farren asked.

Chanel said nothing.

"Well I am, and I know exactly what I got a taste for," she said.

"Why didn't you tell me you knew James?" Chanel asked.

"Does it matter?" Farren asked.

"Yeah it does, I been sitting up with you having all these damn heart-to-heart conversations and you never once mentioned that you knew him and knew him personally," Chanel snapped.

"What do you want to know?" she asked.

"Where is he?" Chanel asked.

"Houston," she said.

"Okay, I wanna see him," Chanel said.

"I thought you wanted to go back to running your business," Farren asked, but in a very sarcastic tone.

"I got this okay, you just drive to get us some food, cus I'm hungry bitch," Chanel said laughing.

"And I need a damn cell phone I am not a prisoner," Chanel snapped.

"You gotta get a trap phone, sorry lil' sis," Farren told her.

"I don't give a damn what it is, I miss Candy Crush."

"Read a book," Farren told her.

"Read a book for what? I don't like reading unless it's a contract," she said.

"I can tell."

"And what the fuck does that mean?"

"Your conversation is limited. You need to start traveling and reading, broaden your horizons," Farren told her.

"Read what? What's your favorite book?" Chanel asked.

"Whew, I don't know, so many to choose from, I love *The Color Purple*," she said.

"I've seen the movie a million times," Chanel brushed her off.

"It's nothing like the movie, girl you are funny, run in there and get you a phone. Here, use cash," she said.

"Why?"

"So no one can trace your whereabouts," Farren said.

"Oh right." Chanel hopped out of the truck and ran into Walgreens. Farren needed to decide what her next move was. She was unsure if she should run up in Chloe's house and get her kids or go talk to James first. James was really the last of the Mohicans left. His counsel would keep her safe and most importantly, alive. James was a part of the original security detail for The Cartel. He had been trained for an extensive amount of time to protect and serve the families who belonged to The Cartel. He stuck by Christian Knight's side and had warned him multiple times about Greg, but Christian was really big on loyalty, and he just knew that his best friend and brother wasn't plotting on him. Lo and behold, it eventually led to his downfall and sadly, his death.

Farren tapped her fingernails on the steering wheel. "Hmmm what to do, what to do," she said aloud.

Her phone rung and it scared her, mainly because nobody ever called her; she was dead. She had gotten this phone a few months ago and it was only to check up on her kids on Chloe's Facebook. No one knew Farren was alive but Mario, her sister, Chanel, James, and now her mother. Farren planned on ducking and dodging up until Greg was taken care of, and after that, she was seriously considering moving to Europe or some other country that was far away.

That's what her and Christian's plans always were upon his retirement from the streets, to move to Africa or London and live like a King and Queen. Christian always complained that Americans were so ungrateful, they didn't appreciate little things like fresh clean water, free education, and most importantly, healthcare. He desired to be around like-minded people like himself, which is why he and Farren traveled so much before having their first child.

"Do we have to go back?" Christian Knight asked his longtime girlfriend.

Farren laughed, but she snuggled closer to him. "Yes, I have a final to study for," she told him.

"Tell him to email it you, that you have a family emergency," he suggested.

"No sir, we've been here long enough," Farren told him. Of course, it was just like Christian Knight to whisk her off to a private island for a few days.

"It's so peaceful here, no service, no emails, no meetings. Just me and the love of my life, smoking and eating good," Christian said, smiling and planting a juicy kiss on Farren's lips.

"Hmmm," Farren moaned.

"What does that sound mean?" Christian acted clueless.

"You already know, don't act," Farren teased.

"Nah I don't, show me," Christian egged her on.

"Now you know that's nothing for me to do," Farren taunted him, pulling the covers back and mounting his lap.

She got comfortable and untied her hair from the bun she pulled it in earlier in the morning. The two lovers had been laid up all day, eating fruit and sipping Champagne. Never in a million years did Farren think her life would be this way, especially with a made nigga such as Christian Knight. He literally catered to her every need. Before she could think or wish for something, she already had it. Christian didn't come with drama, women or lies. She was at peace with him and every single day, a whole new set of emotions were being opened up.

"So you know how to ride?" Christian teased. Farren couldn't ride for nothing in the world, but she loved hopping her thick ass up there.

"Today I do," she said, reaching down and kissing his neck.

Christian pushed her up just a tad bit, so he can slide into her with ease. Farren gasped at him making himself comfortable inside of her. How in the world did it always feel like her first time? She still was unsure, but she never questioned it. Her eyes instantly rolled to the back of her head, and his toes curled. She was in Heaven. Christian rocked her slowly, and she caught on to his rhythm.

"You're my first love," he admitted.

Farren moaned, he was always telling her sweet romantic shit. Farren didn't know if it was all truth but either way it went, Christian always made her feel good. Farren never had to question where his heart was, because Christian never held back how he felt.

"There have been so many before me," she said.

Christian stopped making sweet love to her. He sat up and her boobs met his bare chest.

"Fuck them hoes man," he said.

Farren rolled her eyes; she had heard Dice say that so many times. "Don't roll your eyes. I'm with you and you already know that, so don't even act like that. You're the love of my life; you're smart, you can cook, you got goals, you got your own and don't get me started about how sexy you are. This fat ass...juicy lips... and hmmm...this pussy always tastes sweet." Christian flipped her over and started tickling her.

"Oh my God, stop it, Chrissy!" Farren could barely get it out, she was laughing so hard.

"Nah, don't roll your eyes at me no more," he told her, continuing on.

"Okay...okay! Okay! I promise, I won't ever again," she assured him.

"That's what I thought. Now open your mouth up, let me feel them tonsils." Christian got on his knees and stroked his dick.

He didn't even have to repeat himself. Farren did whatever he asked; she knew how to keep her damn man.

"Farren your phone is ringing!" Chanel yelled, snapping out of her trance.

Farren readjusted herself in the driver's seat, she was sure she had nutted on herself. She hadn't had sex in forever, but she was definitely letting Mario eat her pussy and lick all in her ass every chance she got. He seemed to be satisfied with that, so she was grateful. Farren believed that sex caused too many emotions, and with someone like Mario, she didn't want to even put her spell on him; he wasn't mentally prepared to handle Farren's poison.

Farren saw that Mario had called her seven times in the last few minutes. He had been calling her phone since she turned it back on once they landed back in the states.

"Girl, answer that man's call," Chanel said.

Farren took a deep breath before sliding the bar across with the swipe of her index finger.

"You know I can't talk long," she said.

Mario started in on her ass in Spanish. Farren put the phone on speaker and whipped out of Walgreens parking lot. She dropped the phone in her lap and ignored him while he went on and on in his rant.

"Mario really? That's how you feel?" she finally responded.

Chanel asked, "You know what he is saying?"

"Uh duh, you should always know more than one language," Farren said as if every other black woman walking around Jersey spoke Spanish fluently.

Chanel told herself she had to step her shit up, cus her sister was on it. She just wanted to know did Farren have any flaws, fears, did anything tick her off or make her feel weak or less of a woman cus Chanel could name plenty.

"I'm not...I'm not!" Farren argued with Mario for more than thirty minutes. She pulled up at a barbecue spot and sent Chanel in to get food.

"I got this, I promise you and I will be in contact. We've already been on the phone too long," she told him.

"I don't want you to get hurt. Shit has changed since you been gone, I can't stress that enough," he tried to reason with her.

"I hear you," Farren said. She was tired of having this conversation. She needed rest and meditation to plan her next move.

Mario sighed, "Be safe, I'll be in touch," he told her.

"Okay boo," she told him, so relieved that the call had finally come to an end.

"I'm tired," Chanel told her sister.

"Okay, so do you want to head to Atlanta now or go lay down then leave in the morning?" Farren asked.

"I thought you were going to get your kids?" she asked.

"I'm not sure yet, I need to speak with James and get a second opinion," Farren admitted.

"Well let's just keep it moving cus I miss my daughter," Chanel said. Farren saw the look displayed on her face and it was the same facial expression that she had been having for the last few months.

"I need my babies with me," Farren said, calling her mother.

"Tell my mama to come downstairs in ten minutes," she told her sister and put the phone to her ear.

Farren did an illegal U-turn and headed back to Hardy projects.

Nakia was already in the courtyard when the Escalade came to a complete stop. Of course, Nakia acted like time stopped for her. She finished her conversation, stopped and said hey to a few people before she made her way to the back seat of the truck.

"Damnnnn, we called you thirty minutes ago," Farren said through a mouth full of coleslaw. Oh, how bad did she want a polar sausage with onions!

"Girl shut up," Nakia said. Farren laughed. Chanel didn't understand how Farren always found her mother comical. That lady was fucking evil and mean if you asked her.

"What you need me to do?" Nakia asked.

"Call Chloe, tell her you wanna get the kids to go see me and Christian's graves or something, only cus she'll go for that," she said.

"This late?" Chanel asked.

"You were cremated," Nakia said.

"Cremated? Why?!" Farren questioned.

"Hell, it was cheaper," Nakia told her daughter.

Farren shook her head. "Okay, listen up. if I die for real one day, I want my hair dyed platinum blonde, I want Nikki Martin to do my makeup, she's the truth, bury my ass with fresh mink lashes and I want to have on all-white. I love me some all-white with a brand new pair of red bottoms," she told her family.

"Got you, sis," Chanel said.

Nakia rolled her eyes in the back seat. Chanel was like a little puppet and Farren was so damn bossy it didn't even bother her.

"Okay, so what you want me to say?" Nakia changed the subject. She didn't want to discuss her daughter dying. Nakia knew something was up, she just didn't know what. It was so hard for her to cry and have emotions at the funeral because she knew her daughter wasn't dead. Nakia called it trusting her gut, and as a mother, her heart didn't ache when she heard the news. Nakia played it cool, but when she saw Farren's hips switching through the back of the courtyard from her cameras, it made her damn day. On the inside she was leaping for joy. She didn't pray much, but she was thanking God for answering the few prayers she had got on her knees and prayed, with tears in her eyes and a heavy, forgiving heart.

Nakia would do anything Farren asked to ensure that her daughter was happy. She wasn't the best mom growing up; she hated her past decisions and even how cold she treated Farren because of the hate that had been brewing for her father.

Although Farad did her dirty, she never stopped loving him even when she was pregnant with Farren's sister, Neeki. Farad still loved her. Nakia always knew she wasn't the prettiest, but loyalty outweighed a fat ass and dimples any day. Farad adored Nakia and he waited until he was on his death bed to reveal his true feelings for her. Nakia would cherish that conversation for the rest of her days here on earth.

"Say in the morning but you want them to spend the night because you were already on this side of town," Farren said.

"That might work," Chanel said.

"Okay Ma, give Chloe a call," Farren told her mom.

Nakia pulled out her cellular phone and scrolled through her contacts to call Chloe.

Farren nibbled on her finger; her stomach was in knots, and she felt herself getting sick. She wanted her kids, she just prayed that Chloe's ass wasn't being a bitch.

"Okay, I'm on the way now," Farren's mother said before disconnecting the call.

"Oh my God!" Farren shouted.

"Farren, let me drive and you get in the back seat, your mom can say her car is in the shop and I was giving her a ride home," Chanel suggested.

"Good thinking lil' girl," Nakia said. Everyone switched seats and they made their way to Chloe's house.

"Slow down, make a right," Farren told her from the back seat.

"This isn't Chloe's street," Nakia said.

"I know that, it's my street. I just want to see my house," Farren said.

She gave her sister directions to lead them directly to Farren's old driveway.

"Somebody bought my house," she said sadly.

"This house is the shit," Chanel said, admiring the outer appearance.

"You should have seen the house she had when she and Christian were married, whew," her moms said.

"Let's go," Farren said. Although she had accepted everything that had happened to her in the past few years, the home before her had so many beautiful nightmares. Morgan was conceived in that home, Jonte proposed to her, and sadly, that was where she had "died". The feelings that Farren felt overtaking her body were indescribable. She didn't want to be sad on today; she was finally being reunited with her children, she had made it through the storm.

"I'll be right back," Nakia turned around and told Farren. She smiled and nodded.

Chanel asked her "Are you good sis?"

Farren knew she was going to cry, she couldn't help it, and the waterworks had definitely began.

"I never thought I would see this day," she cried.

Chanel knew how she felt, but the flip side was Farren didn't desert her kids on purpose, or because she was high on drugs. Chanel knew that Madison was too young to remember her mother's dark days, but in the present moment, she promised to never, ever treat her child like that again. Life was too short, and children were blessings from the Creator above. As a person grows older, matriculates through life, and deals with bullshit, they will experience so many different loves, but none will ever compare to the love of a mother. It's the most important relationship a person can have.

Farren clapped her hands together, when she saw how big her son Michael had gotten.

"Look at my fat mama!" Farren said in relations to Morgan. She was growing up to be such a cute little girl. Jonte would be so proud.

Nakia opened the back door, and Noel hopped in first.

"Oh my God!!!!!!!!!!!!!! Mama!!!!!!!!!" she screamed.

Farren put her hands over her daughter's mouth, just in case Chloe was sitting in the window being nosey.

"Shhh baby," she whispered. Farren scooted over, and Noel hopped in her lap, followed by Michael then Morgan. Chanel pulled off as soon as Nakia sat in her chair, the door had barely closed.

"I knew it, Mommy, I knew it," Noel said happily.

Morgan kept rubbing her mother's arm. "Miss you and my daddy," Morgan said.

Farren couldn't stop smiling and crying.

"Michael, you okay?" she asked her son.

Michael laid his head in his lap; he was full of emotion.

"Aww baby, don't cry, Mama is right here, I promise to never leave you again," she covered him.

"I prayed for this day to come every night," Michael said through tears. Farren's heart skipped a beat, her children didn't hate her, they weren't angry. They were really just relieved that they wouldn't be returning to auntie Chloe's house ever again.

"Where were you?" Noel asked.

"At a house getting better because I was very, very sick. I had to learn how to walk all over again," she told her children.

"Like you were a baby again?" Morgan asked.

Farren, Chanel, and Nakia all laughed.

"Yes a baby, I had about thirteen surgeries," Farren told her children. Chanel and Nakia were both unaware of everything that Farren endured, she didn't talk about it. Farren thanked God daily for strength because a few months ago it was a struggle to do anything.

"Can you still cook?" Noel asked.

Farren kissed her daughter's forehead. "Girl yes, what you want to eat?"

Michael spoke, "Pork chops, red beans and rice, and banana pudding," he said, rubbing his stomach.

"And pasta," Morgan shouted.

"And pasta? Okay, I will cook all of it," she said with so much joy.

"Where to now?" Chanel asked.

"We're going to go back to the plane and head to Atl," she said.

"What's in Atlanta?" Noel asked.

"Peace," Farren said and she finally sat back in her seat, relieved.

Chapter 3

"Are you going to see James?" Chanel asked her sister. Farren had spent the last two weeks bonding with her children and making up for as much loss time as possible. It was now time for her to regain focus and handle the mission before her; kill Greg. Greg had to die, there was no IF, AND, or BUTs about it.

Before Farren could respond to her sister, her mother was calling her cell phone.

Farren answered, "What's up mama?" she asked.

"Chloe keep calling my damn phone!" Nakia yelled. Her mother lived a very peaceful life, and with Farren basically kidnapping her children from their legal guardian, Chloe was confused and was threatening to call the police every day.

"I'm about to call her," Farren lied.

"You've been saying that every day, call her or I will," Nakia threatened and hung the phone up.

Farren smacked her lips. Chanel asked again, "Are you going to see James today?"

"Yes I am Chanel, any more questions? How was your day? Mine was fantastic," Farren said sarcastically. They had been staying at Chanel's house. Madison, Morgan, and Noel got along perfect, as if they had knew they were cousins this whole time. Of course, Michael was bored out of his mind, but Farren promised he would be able to call his friends and all of that other stuff that teenagers liked to do, really soon.

"My day was good, meetings on top of meetings, but good," she said, lying across the bed in the guest room, in which Farren had been sleeping.

"I'm going to come and check out your office one of these days," Farren told her.

"You should, I would love that," Chanel told her.

Farren took a deep breath and called her dumb ass sister-in-law, Chloe. Farren didn't fuck with her at all and she stopped pretending a very long time ago to be cordial.

"Chloe, this is Farren, I have my children so no need to keep threatening my mother," Farren said.

She heard Chloe gasp in the phone. "Farren?" she asked for clarification.

"Yes ma'am, I can't chat I'm in the middle of something."

"You have committed fraud; I'm calling the police right now! How dare you take those kids from me. Do you know what those kids have been through?" she shouted.

"Do you know what the fuck I have been through? And Chloe, before you can dial nine-one-one I will have your husband slumped over in his favorite chair," she told her meaning every single word.

"What is wrong with you? You are a devil," she cried.

"Chloe I got shit to do, goodbye," Farren said and disconnected the call.

She tossed her gun in her favorite Louis Vuitton Neverfull MM bag. "Give me like an hour to shower and change, then we can leave, I'll drive" Chanel got off the bed and told her sister.

"You can go next time sweetie, we have important business to discuss," Farren told her, never giving her eye contact.

"No, I'm going," Chanel said.

Farren chuckled, "No you are not," she told her.

"Look, I'm going to say this one time and one time only, you are my sister, not my mother, okay? I raised my damn self. I know you like to think that you struggled and you went through oh so much, but you didn't okay. Until you're running in corner stores stealing sandwiches and juice, you ain't struggled. So like on the real, don't keep talking to me like I'm your assistant. I'm grown as hell, I have a child, and my own business. I'm not making as much as you but it's MY money and I work hard for it. I want to go because I genuinely love you and I'm happy to have you and your kids here. I know I can't help bring Christian Knight back, but I can help. Stop pushing me away, I am not here to hurt you," Chanel told her straight up.

Farren blinked her eyes a few times, trying her hardest not to let her little sister see her cry or get emotional, but Chanel was right. Farren didn't want anyone else getting close to her in fear that they would only betray her or worse, die. She let her guard down with Mari, and look what happened? She partnered up with Greg and he attempted to kill her. Farren was done with females and their pettiness, the lies, the hidden envy, and bullshit. She told herself she was too damn grown for girl's nights in and girl talk too. She had her kids and that's all she needed. Then along came this sister...a sister whom she had never heard about. Chanel kept trying to shower Farren with love and affection, and time after time, Farren pushed her away and treated her cold. This was totally not like Farren. Farren loved her kids so much because of the lack of love she didn't receive at home. Farren was kind and sweet and she told herself in that present moment, she needed to treat Chanel better because at the end of the day, Chanel was really all she had right now. Farren's mother, Nakia, was being secretive, and her other sister, Nikita, had her own bullshit to deal with. Everybody else, who Farren would have normally considered trustworthy, was now dead.

Chanel walked over to her sister and gave her a hug. "I love you and I prayed for this...this bond with you," she told her. She kissed her cheek and went to shower.

Farren looked at herself in the mirror, she wondered had she changed. She knew her physical features had been slightly altered, but spiritually had she changed. Farren was tired of going through shit, seriously. She needed peace, joy, love, comfort, and most importantly, sanity.

"Does he even know we're coming?" Chanel asked.

"I'm trying to stay off the phone as much as possible," Farren told her sister.

"How did you know where he stayed?" Chanel asked yet another question.

"The Cartel," Farren said quickly.

"Well how did you get it from them if they think you're dead?" she asked.

Farren turned around in her seat. "Look, you ask a lot of questions that I don't necessarily know how to answer, shit just happens," she said and turned back around and continued trucking up the hill to James' ranch-styled home. He stayed ducked off in the country, close to the state line of Alabama. When the two women finally approached the home, James was already out there, plucking weeds in the front of his yard.

"Why didn't you just call, I would have drove the golf cart down to get you?" James asked, never taking his attention off his rose bushes.

"Then you wouldn't be surprised to see me," Farren said cheerfully.

"Nothing surprises me anymore, come on," James said seriously. He looked at Chanel but she said nothing, so he didn't either.

James "Blue" Harris, former head of security for the notorious yet elite crime organization, The Cartel, but personal security guard to the infamous Christian Knight. Before realizing that The Cartel was a group of lames and fakes, he paid his way out of the game and relocated to Atlanta, Georgia only to end up back in New York where he opened up a jazz club. James Harris figured Farren Knight would be coming to him soon, he knew she wasn't dead.

James would never forget a conversation that he and Christian Knight had one day when he visited him in prison.

"You know Blue, you're the only person who comes and sees me besides my sister," Christian Knight told him.

"Respect sir," James said. Although they weren't too far apart in age, James respected Christian Knight more than any other man in The Cartel.

"What's on your mind?" Christian detected something was wrong.

"I've decided to leave," James said.

"Why?" Christian asked.

"Shit is not the same," he admitted.

Christian laughed, "Come on now, shit ain't been the same in years."

"Anything you need me to do?" James asked.

Christian shook his head, "Nah fuck all of them, just check on my family from time to time, I'll appreciate that," he said.

"Farren is doing well, I spoke with her the other day," James told Christian.

"Well she hates me, but oh well," Christian said nonchalantly.

"Do you think they'll come after me?" James asked.

"If they do, play dead, that always works," Christian told him seriously.

"You got some sweet tea?" Farren asked.

"No," James said.

"Where were you?" James asked.

"Damn, is that the million dollar question round here," she said sarcastically.

"I looked for you," he said.

"You didn't look hard enough," Farren winked.

"Just don't tell me you were in Atlanta or New York, cus I tore both of them apart."

"Dubai, at Christian's house," she admitted.

"Wow," James said shocked. Farren was the shit; he would never deny that she was one of the smartest women he had ever come into contact with.

"So you've come back to kill Greg and get your seat back?" he asked.

"I came to kill Greg and take over The Cartel," she said.

Chanel spit out her water. "What!"

James shook his head, "You're barely alive, it's all over your face. Were your surgeries even done in a hospital?" James went to lift up her shirt.

She moved out of his way, this motherfucker James wasn't dumb at all.

'I'm good, let's get down to business," she told him, taking a seat at the dining room table.

"What's to discuss, I got an address on him," James said.

"I want it to be done right," she said.

"Look, don't think too hard, this is no game. Keep it simple and kill him. Greg isn't dumb, no need to follow him and all that bullshit, just kill him and do it fast," James told her.

Farren let her head hang. James was taking her twisted fantasy from her, she wanted to make him suffer, but James didn't think any of that was necessary.

"He doesn't get to just go to hell, I need him to see me and regret the day he ever fucked with me," she said with malice in her voice.

"Farren grow up, okay? Kill the motherfucker or I'll do it for you," James said.

"No James, you better not, I will handle it," she told him.

"Cool," he said.

"So after he's dead, is there a protocol you have to follow?" Chanel asked.

James looked irritated with Chanel being in his presence.

"You got something you wanna say nigga?" she asked.

Farren was surprised Chanel was talking to James like that, she clearly didn't know who the fuck he was.

James ignored her. "They have to vote you back in, then you can try and say I wanna be the head. With Bianchi being dead, you might be good. Do you have money to buy your seat back if they ask?" he asked.

Farren smirked, "Now you and I both know money is not an issue," she told him.

"Heyyyy, just asking," James laughed.

Chanel felt her body getting hot; she missed his smile, his touch, everything about him.

"Are you sure this is what you want, to go back to that life?" Chanel asked.

"She never left," James answered for Farren.

"Neither did you," Farren said.

"Oh nah, I'm done, that shit is behind me, I'm too old man, I like my boring life," James told her.

"Come back?" Farren asked.

"Why are you going back?" Chanel was confused.

"I miss the thrill of it," Farren admitted. She hated to say that they sucked her in, but the truth was the truth. She missed the power she felt when she called out the shots.

"I could never do that shit," Chanel said.

"Hey, to each its own," Farren said.

"Well Farren, you've been here before. Me and Chanel are going to lay down for a nap. I'll cook dinner later." James stood and reached his hand out to take Chanel's hand.

Chanel was speechless; Farren couldn't do anything but smile. James was a good man, and although Farren had never met Q, Chanel's sorry ass baby daddy, judging off the way Chanel acted and carried herself, she knew that Chanel could do better.

In Farren's personal opinion, your man or woman was a direct reflection of you, meaning where you lack, they should be able to fulfill. Where you're weak, that should be their strength. A broke motherfucker should not be dating another broke person, two damaged hearts don't belong together. A recovering drug addict shouldn't be laid up with someone who still does drugs; it's like oil and vinegar, it doesn't mix. Dice provided Farren financial support and motivated her to get out of the hood and be better than him. Christian Knight took Farren to a whole nother level; he was a stylish man so it was only right that he upgraded his bitch. Jonte taught Farren how to relax and to be happy. Kool made Farren strong. There is a recurring pattern here. Every relationship that Farren was in, it was beneficial. She didn't believe in wasting her time. Farren didn't deny her infatuation with money, no broke niggas were allowed in her presence. Her little sister had a lot to learn about life, and luckily, she had Farren Knight as her guide to get it together.

Chanel remained quiet as James held her hand and took her to his room. He closed and locked the door, turned around and stared at Chanel. She was still beautiful.

"Hi," he said.

"Hello," she said back.

"How have you been?" he asked.

"Good, I found my sister," she said with a smile.

"I asked about you, not Farren," he told her.

"I'm well," she told him.

"Am I allowed to kiss you?" James asked.

Chanel nodded. James took a deep breath. He bent down and held her face in his hands, before placing one kiss on her forehead, her tiny nose, and then her full lips. Chanel's heart skipped many beats, she had missed that....it had been so long since she felt his touch.

Chanel went to bed every night with James on her mind...she knew that this day was coming, and she was more than ready.

Chanel pulled away from the kiss and told him "I love you."

"I know baby," he said.

"Do you miss me? Have you thought about me?" she asked. Chanel couldn't help that she had always had questions, but hell, she didn't care.

"Yes I have," he told her, going back to savoring the sweet taste of her tongue.

"Hmmm," Chanel moaned. She wrapped her hands around his neck, closed her eyes and enjoyed the passionate kiss.

"Let me shower," James told her.

He handed Chanel a remote control and went to the master bedroom.

Chanel couldn't even concentrate on the show, she knew she needed to be fucked. She came out of her clothes and tiptoed into the bathroom and pulled the shower door back.

"Nine minutes and forty two seconds," he said.

Her eyebrows rose in confusion, "Huh?"

"It took you too long to come to me, I don't like waiting," he told her.

"I'm sorry, how can I make it up to you baby?" she asked toying with her nipples. Chanel knew she was about to fuck her weave up, but she didn't care, James's dick was worth it.

"Let me see if you still know how to make me cum only using your tongue," he suggested.

Chanel didn't have to be told twice. James moved the shower head to the wall and Chanel got on her knees slowly taking his love muscle into her mouth.

"Ooh," he jumped at her touch. Her mouth was so warm and wet. Chanel didn't take her time, she instantly started sucking him fast and fondling his balls.

"Damn ma," he hissed.

She made slurping noises and caused her tonsils to lightly vibrate on his dick. She decided to be a big girl and open her eyes and watch James enjoy his head, and the sight before her caused her hands to somehow find their way between her legs. Chanel was making her pussy feel so good she started hopping on the floor, riding her fingers causing herself to squirt and cum all over the granite floor in the shower.

James picked her up and Chanel stuck her fingers down his throat, he sucked them hungrily.

"Damn, that pussy still tastes like that?" he asked.

She nodded, kissing all over his neck and rubbing her hands up and down his back.

"Can I stick it in?" James teased her.

"Please," she begged.

James pushed her against the wall and rubbed his dick against her clit. "Look at all that cream on my dick," he said surprised.

Chanel was creaming and it seemed as if her pussy wouldn't stop it.

"James, stop playing and fuck me man," she said getting frustrated and tired of him running it up and down her clit.

James didn't want to upset his baby love, so he inserted his penis into her tight pussy and stroked her slowly. He closed his eyes and savored the moment. James was thankful for this. He had been working out all day and this was the perfect way to end his Monday afternoon, fucking the woman of his dreams.

"I'm about to cum," she moaned.

"Already?" he asked, speeding up his pace.

"I haven't had sex in a year," she told him.

"Damn, for real ma? So this still my pussy?" he asked, stroking her real good.

"Yes, you know that," she said whimpering at his touch.

James loved her statement. He pulled out of her and went down below and began feasting on Chanel's pretty lil' pussy. Her hair was soaking wet but she didn't care. James was putting a beating on her pussy. He wouldn't stop licking her even after she had screamed "I'M CUMMING" more than three times.

Once he was satisfied, he pulled the showerhead in their direction and held her waist tight as Chanel cleaned and rinsed their bodies.

"Come on, we gotta get out," she laughed. James was on her like white on rice.

"Why are you so beautiful?' he asked, kissing on her neck.

"You think so for real?" she asked.

James looked at her and smiled. She had the tiniest moles decorating her face and only one who stared at her for a long period of time would notice. Her eyelashes were long on the bottom and thick and short on the top. Her nose was tiny but it was wide, her teeth were perfect except one tooth on the right but James didn't care. Chanel's birthmark was the shape of Texas right above her collarbone. She had beautiful hair but chose to wear weave. She was tall and her figure was to die for. Not only that, but she valued a dollar and worked hard for everything she had. This woman was designed for James.

"You're everything I've been looking for," he told her.

Chanel hugged him. She knew he meant every word and her heart told her it was okay to love him, so with no setbacks or hesitations, she wanted to give him her all.

"Come on let me dry you off," James told her, stepping out the shower.

An hour later, they laid in bed staring at each other, catching up on the past year.

"How are you and Farren doing?" he asked.

Chanel smiled. James noticed the glow she had and he was happy that she got what she always wanted, family.

"She's bossy as hell but she means me well," she told him.

"Just remain you," he told her.

"What made you say that?" Chanel asked.

"I don't want you getting caught up in anything that's all," he said.

"She's not going to let that happen."

"I didn't say she would, I'm telling you to remain focused on your own goals baby," James told her. He needed Chanel to learn how to listen and take what he said for what it was instead of trying to analyze everything.

James watched Chanel doze off, and once he knew she was sleep, he threw some gym shorts on and a V-neck and went to talk to Farren.

"I made spaghetti," she said when he came into the kitchen.

"My mama always said 'never eat a black woman's spaghetti'," he joked.

"How have you been James, seriously?" Farren asked.

"I'm living," he told her.

"My sister really likes you."

James ignored her statement. He and Chanel's relationship would never be up for discussion, he was an extremely private person.

"Greg is living in Arizona. I don't know what it is about that state, but he loves it there," James said.

"The girl he really, really fucks with lives there," she said nonchalantly.

"I thought he was in love with Courtney, Christian's sister?" he asked.

"He probably was, but his WIFE is in Arizona."

"Wife?" James asked.

"Yep, wife."

"And how do you know this?"

"They got married about two years after me and Chrissy did, it was just us four in Vegas," Farren said.

"Smart nigga," James said. That's something that he would have done too.

"Yeah, Greg wasn't no dummy, I will give him that."

"And you plan on killing her too?" he asked.

"Fuck no."

"Have you spoken with anyone in The Cartel? How is everything going?

"Yes I have," she said.

"Who?" James asked.

Farren looked agitated with James numerous questions, "Mario."

"Sanchez?"

"Yes and before you start, I don't even wanna hear it," she told him, getting up to wash her plate out.

"Hey you're grown, do you," James told her.

"It's not like that. You really think I would do that?" Farren came back into the dining room and asked. She was in defense mode.

"Why are you so riled up?" he teased.

"I didn't fuck him!" she said.

"If you didn't go that far, y'all did something; it's all in your demeanor."

"How soon should I go kill Greg?" she changed the subject.

"Tomorrow," he stated.

"Yep, it's murking season," James smiled sinisterly.

Farren sat in the dining room chair. She couldn't believe the time had come.

"He took so much from me."

"In and out," he reminded her.

"I know, I know," she fanned him away.

James walked back to his bedroom. Farren sat in the dining room chair the entire night, tapping her nails on the table in serious deep thought. It wasn't fair, life was not fucking fair.

Farren would never forget how she felt staring at Christian's body at the morgue. It took everything for her to enter the actual room where his body lay on the cooling board.

"You want me to go with you?" Jonte asked.

"No, no I'm okay baby," she told him, weakly.

Farren walked into the room, and she couldn't take any more steps towards him. Christian lay there, appearing to be relieved.

"You weren't supposed to leave me like this," she said from the corner of the room.

Her heart was breaking and her tears were silent. Her sobs made no noise, Farren held her stomach. "It's not fair," she shook her head.

"You promised me forever!" she yelled.

"Why Christian? Why did you have to fuck that girl and mess up our happy life?" she carried on.

Farren knew she had to get it all out, "I loved you with everything in me and you left me."

"I was the perfect wife and you still didn't love me like I loved you."

"I tried to move on Chrissy, I tried my hardest, but they never compared to you...never." she told him.

Farren wiped her tears...she was alone. Everyone went back to their normal lives after the funeral. People only called for a few weeks, but eventually the calls and balloons stop coming, even the pastor stops praying for you. Farren mourned on her own, she got herself together by herself.

"You okay sis?" Chanel asked, peeping into the room with one of James t-shirts on top of her naked body.

Farren wiped her tears, "Yeah, you enjoyed herself?" she asked smiling.

Chanel smiled back. Farren was looking like she was really going through something, she just wished that her sister would talk about it.

"Yes I did, you cooked?" Chanel asked.

"Yeah spaghetti, this nigga James got all the food," she joked.

"His house is beautiful," she added.

"I love ranch-styled homes," Farren said.

"Hmmm, this is good," Chanel said after she joined her sister at the table.

"I haven't made spaghetti in years, my kids got expensive taste, lamb and shit," Farren said.

"Girl, I've never had lamb before," Chanel told her.

"Are you serious? Girl I make the best lamb chops in the world," Farren boasted.

"Nah, what they taste like?" Chanel asked.

"I'm going to make you some sis," she said.

"I prayed for you," Chanel told her.

"Why?" Farren asked.

"I want you to be happy."

"My kids make me happy."

"My daughter does too, but still, that's not what love I'm talking about," she said.

"I live a very private life, I don't have time to meet somebody, I'm too secretive. I think everybody is the FEDS," Farren told her.

"You need to date a teacher or something, a man with some patience."

"A teacher? How much they make a year?" Farren frowned up her nose.

"It's not always about money," Chanel told her.

"In my book and in between my legs, yes it is."

"But why, if you have your own money?"

"It just does, I like stability and security."

"But you can protect yourself," Chanel said.

"And my man needs to be able to protect me too," Farren told her.

"Let me share this with you. My ex, Morgan's daddy, Jonte...let me see... I'm forty-seven now, Jonte was like thirty-four or five when I met him. I can't remember, but he ain't have much girl. He had a nice car and all that but he spent everything he made, no bank account or nothing. I had wayyyy more than Jonte did but girl, that man loved everything about me down to my dirty draws," Farren said.

"Where is he now?" Chanel asked.

"He died, somebody killed him to get to me," she said. Chanel couldn't imagine all what Farren had really been through.

"Are you for real?"

"Yes, I'm serious. He died no less than three weeks after Christian died," she said.

"Who killed him?"

Farren looked at her... "KIM!"

She forgot to add Kim to her list, that bitch had to go.

How in the world did she forget to avenge Jonte's death? Too worried about Christian Knight. Farren now felt really bad, so Kim would be dying first.

"I miss him," she ignored Chanel's question.

"Did y'all get married?" she asked.

"Nah, but we were engaged. I don't think I'll ever get married again, waste of money. Weddings are for show, you can get married for twenty-five dollars at the courthouse."

"I don't have no family, I just wanna go to some nice ass island and get married," Chanel said.

"Me and Chrissy renewed our vows on the beautiful island in Barbados, just me and him," Farren said with so much glimmer in her eyes.

"I want to experience that one day," Chanel said.

"What?"

"Love, real love."

"It's hard to keep. The first ten years of marriage is the hardest, I don't a give a damn what nobody says," Farren said.

"Why the first ten years?"

"You really don't know that nigga when y'all are dating, but once you live with someone every single day for ten years straight...marriage is about compromise. Marriage has to be a partnership. I allowed my husband to lead, but at the end of the day, we were a team," she schooled her sister.

"So do you regret marrying him?"

"CHRISTIAN KNIGHT? Hell nah! He made me who I am."

"I don't know if I can ever give a man that much credit," Chanel said.

Farren didn't give a damn how her sister felt, her or anybody else. Christian Knight was the shit, point blank period.

"I owe him so much, I was so broken when I met him," she said.

"That's how I feel about James," Chanel admitted.

"Well don't run him away and cut that other nigga off."

"Why do you keep bringing him up, he's irrelevant," she snapped.

"Now if you think that then you haven't learned anything from me so far," Farren told her.

"What does that mean?" Chanel was confused.

"Chanel, you need to start listening and thinking before you ask questions," Farren said.

James entered the room. "I keep telling her that."

"Okay, we're not about to gang up on me," Chanel said.

"We're family, no gang up needed. But for real, you are a smart girl, please start acting like it. I'm going to lay down. James, you stay too damn far, where is the guest room?" she asked.

James showed her to a bedroom.

Farren laid down and called Chanel's grandmother to check on the kids, and she said they were all outside in the yard playing. Knowing her kids were straight, Farren decided to lie down and take a nap.

The next morning, Chanel awakened up to James's head buried in between her legs.

"Hmm, good morning," she moaned.

James stopped and said "good morning," as he came up and kissed her passionately. Chanel loved tasting herself. She sucked on his tongue before pushing his head down right back where it belonged.

"Oh yes, aah," she squealed. Chanel began to bring her pussy into his mouth. James didn't have to do much but keep his tongue stiff like a tiny surfboard.

Minutes later, she came and was satisfied. James went to wash his self up and brush his teeth before returning to wash Chanel's middle up.

"Come on, I made some muffins and coffee," James told Chanel.

"Let me go get Farren," she told him.

The bedroom door to the room that she slept in was closed, so Chanel knocked before entering. Chanel knocked a few times and after not hearing her say "come in" she opened the door and saw that the bed was made up as if no one had ever slept in it the night before.

Chanel went to the kitchen and asked James "Where is Farren?'

"She's not in the room?" he asked.

She shook her head. "Check the bathroom," he suggested.

Chanel returned minutes later. "She's not in there nor is she answering the damn phone," she said frustrated.

"She will be back, don't worry about her. I'll take you home later on today," he told her handing a coffee mug.

James was entirely too calm.

"You know where she is don't you," she said with her hands on her hip.

He smiled and kissed her cheek.

"You're so adorable," James told her.

"Adorable my ass, that's my sister James," she said.

James laughed, "I've been knowing Farren way longer than you, almost twenty-five years," he said.

"We are blood," she clarified.

"Okay baby." James didn't want to argue with her.

"She's not mentally stable," Chanel said.

"What you mean?"

"I never see her sleep, whenever a door opens she jumps, she totes a gun in her robe, some days her breathing is short then she said her back be hurting. She thinks no one hears her crying at night but her kids hear her," she said.

James remained quiet, just taking it all in. He noticed that Farren wasn't in tip-top shape either, and he wondered if maybe she wasn't ready to kill Greg.

"I'll be back," James said dashing out of the kitchen.

"Huh? What? Wait!" she said running after him. She searched the halls until she found James in what looked like an office, until she saw him pressing buttons under his desk, which caused bookshelves to turn around and display all types of guns.

"James what the fuck is this?"

"You really don't know who you're dealing with...me and Farren live in a different world than you do, I warned you about this," he told her moving around the room loading guns.

"I want to be in it," she said.

"No the fuck you don't, you see what she went through!" he yelled.

"She lost her husband okay, people lose their husband every day," Chanel said nonchalantly.

James looked at her disappointed. "What?" Chanel asked.

"I lost more than my husband...James are you coming with me?" Farren asked.

Chanel turned around.

"Farren, I didn't know you were here, I thought you left," she said.

She smiled at her, but it was one of those 'bitch, you done fucked up' smiles.

"I went running," she said.

"Give me ten minutes," James said.

"Five," Farren told him and walked off.

"You said she was gone," Chanel fussed.

"I said I knew where she was going," he told her.

"She hates me."

"No she doesn't, but you have to be more sensitive and careful, she's not right in the head," James told her truthfully.

"When will y'all be back?" she asked.

"I don't know, but you should go home with the kids," he told her walking out of the room.

Chanel went and put her clothes back on. James and Farren were in the dining room looking over a paper when Chanel reentered the kitchen.

"Farren, I'm about to head back to Atlanta and take the kids somewhere and do some work for one of my clients," she said.

Farren didn't say anything. James went over and walked her to the door. "Call me when you get home so I can know you made it safe. When I get back it's a few things I'm going to show you," he told her.

"Like what?" she asked.

James kissed her forehead, "How to survive in these streets," he stated seriously.

"I don't have your number," she added.

"I have yours; I'll call you in an hour."

"Or you can text me."

"I'm old school baby, I want to hear your voice," James causing Chanel to blush.

After Chanel was off the premises, Farren already had the guns loaded up and she was able to pull a similar blueprint of Greg's home, due to the builder of his subdivision having the layout available on the internet.

"You ready?" James asked.

"Yeah, let's ride," Farren replied.

"You wearing that?" he asked. Farren had on a long summer dress with sandals.

"Uh yeah."

"Nah, you need some all black. What, your husband didn't teach you anything?" James teased.

"Ugh, okay, okay," Farren whined.

As they traveled down the road, Farren turned the radio down. "We flying right?" she asked.

"I wasn't planning on it, but we can," he told her.

"Uh, yeah nigga."

"I have a detour to make anyway," she said.

"And where would that be Farren?" James asked.

"I gotta slide on down to the 305."

"What's there? Mario?" he laughed.

"No, I gotta kill Kim's ass," she stated seriously.

"You on a roll ain't you."

"Farren Knight is back," she said before sliding her designer shades over her dark eyes.

Chapter 4

"Okay the wife just got home, you ready?" James asked.

Farren nodded. Her heart was racing, adrenaline pumping, but she had never been so ready in her life. James drove the car around the neighborhood a few more times, trying to peep anything that was out of the ordinary.

"James coast is clear, let's get this shit over with," she said annoyed.

"Hey, my life is on the line just like yours is, we both know this motherfucker Greg ain't wrapped too tight," James said.

He slowly turned the truck onto the road that Greg and his wife lived on once more, before deciding to park in the driveway of a house that was for sale. To anyone peeping from their windows, James and Farren appeared to be a happy, newly married couple, looking to find their dream home to start their life together and have children.

James and Farren held hands as they crossed the street, dressed in all black and ready to motherfucking kill.

Farren wanted to bust in the house and tie Tonya's ass up, but James had other plans. He knocked on the door and waited to hear Greg's wife voice.

"Who is it?" she asked.

"Hi ma'am, my name is Carter Young, I'm new to the area. Do you by any chance know where the mailboxes are located?" he asked in a fake Southern accent.

Seconds later, the door was being unlocked and the two were greeted by a big smile.

Tonya's smile went stoned. "Farren what are you doing here?" she asked.

Farren didn't bother responding. She marched her way into the home and James followed in, locking the door.

Tonya ran to grab the house phone.

"Tonya, I'm not here to kill you, I actually came to have girl talk," Farren told her, after she shot the silencer in her direction.

James spoke, "The next time she won't miss, so sit down."

"Farren, we are family, why are you here and I thought you died?"

"Well if I did die and we are supposed to be family, why weren't you at my funeral sweetie?" she said.

"Greg was out of town on business, you know I don't come to Jersey without him," she stuttered.

"Tonya, did you know that Greg killed Christian? My husband, the father of my children," Farren asked.

Her eyes got big, "What?"

"Yep, why do you think he's been home so much lately? I mean, come on now, we both know Greg was only here on holidays or when you threatened to leave."

Tonya said nothing, because Farren wasn't telling anything but the truth. He told her that he wanted to work on their marriage and he realized that she was really the one for him. Tonya had done a little lurking on social media. She knew that Courtney, Greg's real love, had killed herself. Truth of the matter was, ever since then, Greg had never been the same. She never questioned his sudden return to Arizona to be with her, didn't ask any questions when he changed the locks and their phone numbers, didn't mumble a word when he strategically left guns all over the house and told her how to evacuate in case of an emergency.

Tonya wasn't the brightest apple in the bunch, but she damn sure wasn't a dummy. She knew the life that Greg lived wasn't a safe one, but he was all she'd ever known. Greg was a quiet and mysterious man, that's what originally attracted her to him. Tonya worked hard to gain Greg's attention and most importantly, his time. She chased his ass down for a few years before he finally decided to give her his last name. Tonya never expected much out of Greg. The nigga didn't even propose, he asked her to become his wife during a steamy fuck session and she moaned "Yes."

Greg crushed her dreams of having a fairytale wedding and told her she didn't need to have her friends there, when she confessed her love and promised to be there for Greg 'til infinity. She never objected; she was so happy that he was giving her the ring.

Tonya only ended up being more disappointed when she kept asking where her wedding ring was and Greg handed her a knot of money and told her to get whatever she wanted. When she asked what color wedding band he wanted, he laughed and said he wasn't wearing no damn wedding ring, she better be happy he was even paying for a ceremony.

Tonya never rolled her eyes, never cursed at him, never cheated; she stayed by his side in hopes that one day something would change.

"Why would he kill Christian?" she asked.

"The same reason he tried to kill me, he's greedy and selfish," Farren told her.

"What time does he normally get home?" James asked, after he had searched the entire home and had removed all weapons.

"Not sure, I can call him though," she offered.

Farren was surprised and Tonya noticed her facial expressions.

"Just don't kill me, I will tell you the code to the safe and everything."

"Why?" James asked.

"I haven't been happy in years. This is a sign from God telling me to leave and find my own happiness," she said with tears in her eyes.

Farren knew how that felt, she knew that look all too well. It hurts to admit that your husband doesn't love you as much as you love him, it's painful.

We as women love too hard, we try too hard and we ignore the signs for so long, until your man basically holds the sign up to you and it reads, "I DO NOT LOVE YOU ANY MORE!"

We're then stuck, confused, lost, frozen and in a daze. We try to put the pieces of the puzzle back together. We have questions and they never seem to have the answers. We want to know is it because we gained weight or don't ride the dick for as long as we used to? Is it another woman? Is it you? Is it me? How in the world do we fix this? Who wants to leave the one you gave your heart to? The one you love and want to spend the rest of your life with? No one does. It's not fair! Love is so beautiful, but oh does that motherfucker hurt. It will kill you if you let it.

Tonya called Greg and asked him when he was coming home because she was about to start cooking dinner.

Greg responded. "I'm pulling up now, I left my other phone but I'm just running in bae."

Tonya looked scared. Farren appeared ready and James didn't move from where he stood. This was nothing to him, fear didn't run through his blood. James had killed so many niggas in his day, this would be a piece of cake if this was his mission, but it wasn't. Farren wanted the body on her hands, he was just here to assist if need be.

They went and sat in the living room, catching up. Farren whispered to Tonya, "This will be over in less than five minutes."

James was standing behind a wall in the dining room, observing. He had heard about how well Farren had been trained. Jeff and James were brothers, which were one of the reasons why James wanted to kill Greg, but he had been told his brother to stop fucking with The Cartel. However, he was hardheaded. He loved the money and the supposed power that came along with The Cartel. His pride and joy had become Farren Knight. Jeff used to call James and boast about how he was whipping Farren into becoming one of the baddest bitches in The Cartel.

"Baby?" Greg shouted out.

"In here," Tonya said, her voice was shaky.

"Why you sound like th-" Greg stopped mid-sentence when he saw Farren Knight sitting on his motherfucking Italian leather couch.

Greg went to grab his gun but before he could even pull it out of his jeans, Farren had shot a hole in his hand.

"Fuck!" Greg winced.

James got a hard on instantly; this bitch Farren was on it.

"Nah, get up pussy ass nigga," she got up and walked over to him.

Farren turned her back so she could see Tonya and Greg, although James was near, Farren still was covering herself. She had trust issues, and ain't no telling what ill feelings James was probably harboring.

"Tonya, if you try any funny shit I'm going to shoot the shit out of you," she warned.

Tonya shook her head.

Greg asked, "You trifling bitch, you set me up."

"Shut up, no she didn't, but she should have. You don't deserve her, hell, you don't deserve anybody," Farren kicked him on his back and shot him in both of his kneecaps.

"You came back...yeah you did. I'll give you that, but you should have made sure my heart wasn't beating," Farren spit in his face.

James was watching the timer on his watch; Farren was doing all this talking when he clearly told her in and out.

"You came into my house to kill me!!!!!!" she kicked him again.

Farren wanted to cry just thinking of that horrid day; she just knew that she was going on to Glory.

Farren felt her heartbeat slowing down, her head felt like it had been hit on each side with a baseball bat. Actually that wasn't a good enough description, the pain was indescribable. She couldn't believe she had been caught slipping. Her eyes struggled to stay open, and it was as if God sent the Angel Gabriel to her. She saw a body standing over her, and she just knew that this motherfucker came back to shoot her once more just to make sure she was dead for real. Farren's eyes were filled with blood and tears, her vision was extremely blurry and before she knew it, she had passed out from the lack of blood.

On the way to the hospital, the person who rescued her, Mario, sat in the back of the ambulance. He asked, "Is there any way you can take this truck somewhere else?"

"What do you mean?" they asked. They were already working extremely hard to keep her alive, but her body had suffered too much damage. Along with the consumption of pills and alcohol, Farren Knight was on thin ice.

"I have money, I can pay," he tried to reason.

"I'm not going to jail and who let him in the truck?"

"I don't have a problem killing you and driving this bitch myself."

"What do you want?"

"I will pay you to keep her alive but she can't go to the hospital," he asked.

"She is in no condition to travel."

"She's a fighter."

"Sir, we keep losing her, can you please let us do our job?" the man yelled.

Mario banged his hand on the wall on the inside of the truck. Farren couldn't go to the hospital, she just couldn't.

"You might as well kill me bitch," Greg laughed.

"Of course I'm going to kill you but you owe me an explanation."

James walked in the room, "You doing too much, kill this motherfucker."

Greg was surprised. "Well if it isn't Christian's bitch boy, what you doing playing captain save-a-hoe, I thought The Cartel was too much for you?"

In the midst of him about to die, he was still talking shit. Farren saw Greg reaching for his gun with his other hand and she shot him quickly.

"Finally," James spat.

Farren reached down to make sure he was dead but for good measure, she shot his ass two more times.

James came behind her and shot his ass up some more.

Farren was good and all, but she had a lot to learn about tucking emotions and staying focused on the task at hand. If she wasn't careful, she would end up dead the next time. Tonya had thrown up all over herself. She looked horrible, but then again, Farren knew exactly what that looked like; seeing the man you love, no matter how much bullshit he put you through, dead. Damn, it really did something to you.

Farren knew that look all too well.

She was mad that Greg didn't suffer or apologize before dying, but he was dead. That was one thing knocked off her to-do list.

"Tonya, you didn't see us did you?" Farren asked.

She shook her head. "Good," Farren responded.

James couldn't believe the ignorance of Farren, he turned around and killed her instantly.

"Why the fuck did you do that, I promised her I wouldn't kill her," she yelled.

"Go get your ass in the car," he told her calmly. Farren was stuck in the place she stood. James pointed the gun at her, "Car" he said again.

She made her way to the car, checking her surroundings for anything out of the ordinary, but the coast was clear.

About twenty minutes later, James returned to the vehicle and started it up without saying one word.

"Everything straight back there?" Farren asked.

James nodded. Farren peeped the attitude but she didn't know why he had one.

"Is there an issue James?" she asked.

"You have a lot to learn and you don't listen, and it's crazy to me because after all of the shit you have been through, you're still fucking stupid."

"Excuse me?"

"You was about to let that lady live. What loyalty does she owe to you? You just killed her husband, the husband who before you told her how sorry he was, she really didn't have a clue."

"I know how it feels to be with someone."

"There are no feelings in this shit!" he banged on the steering wheel. James felt himself getting riled up and that's not what he wanted. This is why he got out of The Cartel. He cared too much, too concerned. James was entirely too passionate about his job and the people he was paid to protect.

"I'm sorry," she mumbled sadly.

Farren really wasn't sorry. James had no idea the bullshit, the hurt, the pain, the misery that she faced dealing with the death of her estranged husband, Christian Knight. The memories, the moments, the shared celebrations and accomplishments, it was if they went down the drain once Farren saw Christian Knight's body lifeless in that bed.

Greg stole her happiness away. Although Farren was madly in love with Jonte, men like Christian Knight captured your heart forever. She wasn't able to accept that he was gone. While Farren was resting in that abandoned home, she remembered telling Mario,

"Dubai," she whispered.

"Huh?" he said. Farren didn't talk much. The emergency attendants that he had kidnapped told him that she had most likely suffered memory loss. Mario was panicking and didn't know what else to do, Farren had lost so much weight. They warned him that she needed better care or she would be dying very soon.

"Dubai...Chrissy," she said before falling back asleep.

Mario didn't know anything about being in Dubai. He searched through a private directory that only The Cartel had access to. His fingers scanned through the "Medical" section. He was hoping that one of these doctors were familiar with the Knight's.

He closed his eyes and prayed in Spanish before making a few calls. One doctor in particular was so disturbed by the news, he dropped the phone and Mario waited for almost twenty minutes for him to return the call.

He asked to speak to the nurses who were overseeing Farren.

They passed the phone back to Mario. "She is not doing well from what I have heard, I'm not sure if a flight is even suitable. Christian Knight was one of my favorite people… how about this, I fly over there with my staff and we patch her up and bring her back," he suggested.

"Umm okay…please don't make any phone calls about this."

"I've been doing this for years, I know how it goes. See you soon," he said and disconnected the call.

"Hold on just a lil' bit longer," he whispered in her ear.

James had no idea what Farren had gone through. Greg didn't get what he deserved. He needed more. She wanted him to suffer and die wishing he had never crossed the Connect's Wife.

"Don't be sorry, be careful."

They made it back to Atlanta safely. "Are you still going with me to handle Kim?" she asked.

"I think you need to get some sleep and go to the doctor because you look like shit."

"It's the pills," she admitted.

"Pills?" he asked.

"I'm off of them and my body is going through withdrawals."

"Farren, your surgeries were botched, you need to go see a doctor, save the bullshit about the pills, you been taking them for years," James told her and unlocked the door, which signified he was ready for her to get out of his car.

"Tell Chanel I will call her later," he said. Farren didn't bother responding. James had kind of gotten on her nerves these last three days.

She walked in the house and was just a tad bit grateful no one was there but Chanel's grandmother.

"Hello," Farren spoke.

Her grandmother said, "Hi" back.

"Where are the children?" she asked.

"White Waters."

"By themselves?" Farren asked.

"You didn't expect me to take them did you?" her grandmother asked sarcastically.

"No, but they could have waited on me, they're not old enough to be anywhere by themselves."

"You can't baby them forever chile," she said and took her attention back to her soap operas.

Farren thought she was about to come take a shower and get some rest, but she turned on her heels and went to Chanel's garage and hopped in her Honda.

On the highway, Chanel's engine light kept flashing.

"Oh nah, I gotta go to the dealer today and get me a house TODAY," Farren said to herself.

Chanel's grandmother mouth was a little too much for Farren and all she cooked was starchy foods. Farren was a health nut.

She called Michael's phone three times before he finally answered.

"Wassup ma?" he said.

"Come on out to the front, I'm pulling up in Auntie Chanel's car," she said.

"Aww man, we were in line for the biggest slide they had," he said angrily.

"We can come back tomorrow or this week, I promise," she told him.

"Man, come on y'all, mama outside," Michael said.

"Stay on the phone with me," Farren told him.

She was paranoid as fuck and didn't play about her children. She would have appreciated if Chanel or her grandmother would have called and asked if it was okay if her kids went to a public water park with thousands of people without any adult supervision, but they didn't .

"Why did we have to leave?" Noel asked when they got in the car.

"Hi to you too, child."

"I was having fun mommy," Morgan said. Farren turned around and smiled at her child. "Where are her sandals?" she asked.

"I don't know," Noel said shrugging her shoulders.

"Hi Madison," Farren spoke to her niece.

"Hi auntie," she said smiling.

"Do y'all want to move into a house or a condo like me and Daddy had?" Farren asked.

"Condo, they got a pool and food," Michael said.

"I cook and you acting like y'all never had a pool."

"I want a big doll house," Morgan said.

"Noel, what about you?" Farren asked her daughter.

"It don't matter to me, I just want my own room, Morgan pees in the bed."

"Huh?" Farren said.

"She's always peeing," Noel said. She wasn't used to sharing a room, let alone a bed, but when the children were placed in Chloe's custody, they had to sleep in one bed. Morgan cried every night for her mommy and daddy and peed the entire time. Chloe got tired of getting out of her bed to give her a bath and rock her to sleep, so she told Noel don't come in her room no more waking her up. So Noel was forced to sleep on a pissy mattress until the next morning. She had started sleeping in the bed with Michael, until Chloe whooped her so bad one night and told her girls and boys don't sleep in the same bed. Noel cried because she, Carren, and Mike used to sleep in the same bed all the time.

"Morgan, you okay baby? You want to still be a baby and wear diapers?" she asked.

Morgan shook her head no.

Farren's children needed counseling; they never really discussed everything that happened with Christian and Jonte. Farren felt badly for not talking to her kids, she was dealing with their deaths too, but still, her children's feelings should have come first.

"Well house it is," Farren said changing the subject.

"Is it going to have a basement?" Michael asked.

"NO!" Farren shouted.

Michael looked at his mama and wondered what he said to cause her to yell.

"No basement baby, I'm sorry," she said.

Farren was terrified of basements now; she didn't like how you couldn't really hear anything that goes on upstairs. She was done with basements but she would try her hardest to build Michael the perfect teenager man's cave because that's all he really wanted, his own space away from his annoying sisters.

Once the family returned home, Farren spent the rest of the night looking at houses. Being that she had nothing, she knew she would be doing her favorite thing for the next few days, shopping.

She was excited. Farren loved taking nothing and turning it into something. She emailed a realtor using Chanel's name and set up a few appointments for tomorrow. She already knew she was buying a Range Rover and a Bentley Coupe. Farren always had to have at least two options when waking up in the morning and opening the door to her garage. Depending on what mood she woke up in, Farren might just purchase more than two.

She needed to get her kids enrolled in something productive for the summer and school in the Fall. She also needed to find something to do with her time besides seeking revenge on those who crossed her. Farren looked over at her calendar and the date was April 29. She had less than three months to get ready for The Roundtable. Farren planned to pop up in there and switch shit up. She needed to stay on Mario's good side so she can stay in the loop of what's going on.

She called his cell phone, the phone he had for her and her only.

"Hola," he said dryly.

"I miss you," she said.

"Come to Miami then," he told her.

"I can't, I have a lot going on right now."

"Alright, I'm happy to hear you're doing well. Take care Farren," he said and hung the phone up.

Farren took a few deep breaths before pressing his name once again on her phone.

The phone rang a few times and Mario finally answered.

"I'm in the middle of something and you're playing games," he said.

Farren rolled her eyes. Mario was so childish. This is what he wanted from her, to blow him up and beg for a few seconds of his time. This kind of shit didn't mean a person loved or cared about you, but Mario was still young, he didn't know any better, so Farren played right along with his ass.

"I want to see you," she whined.

"Okay, so come to Miami."

"Why can't you come here for a few days?"

"I'm in the middle of business, you know it's about to be the first of the month." Farren knew that much to be true. The first and end of the month were extremely crucial for anyone dealing with and supplying drugs.

"I'll fly out tomorrow night," she told him.

"Cool," he said and hung the phone up. Mario was done being nice to Farren's ass, she had been taking his kindness for weakness for far too long.

Farren went to check on her sister. "Hi, how was your day?" she asked.

"It was good, I'm tired," she said yawning.

"I hear it in your voice. Well me and the kids will be out of here in a few days," she told her sister.

Chanel looked extremely sad. "Why? What's wrong?"

"Girl nothing, just ready to get back in my own house and cook and stuff," she said.

Chanel saw the uneasiness in Farren's face. "Everything okay?" she asked.

"Yeah, yeah, everything is good, we still going to see each other Chanel. I might stay close by so Noel and Morgan can still come and play with Madison," she said.

Chanel smiled, that made her feel better. She didn't want her newfound family to go too far.

"Okay cool," she said.

"I'm going to Miami this weekend, you down?"

"I never been," she said.

"Girl, what? Oh yeah, you're going," Farren told her.

"I gotta see if that's in my budget, you know it's the first of the month," Chanel said opening her Wells Fargo app.

"Don't worry about anything, we gone have fun shopping and eating," she said.

Farren saw her phone ringing. It was a 281 number and she didn't recognize the area code so she didn't answer.

Her mother called seconds later. "Girl what do my mama want?" she said aloud while her and Chanel looked at hotels and stuff.

"We can stay at Mario's house," she told her sister before answering the phone.

"That's your sister calling you," Nakia said as soon as Farren answered.

"Oh shit, I know she's mad," Farren said. She instantly felt bad about not letting her sister know she was still alive.

"Mmm hmm," she said.

"Ma, you work this weekend? You wanna go to Miami?" she asked.

Chanel frowned up her face.

"Uh, no I don't," her mother said.

"Why?"

"Because Farren, I don't have babysitter tattooed to my damn forehead," she said.

"Bye ma," Farren said smacking her lips and rolling her eyes.

"Bye heffa."

"I'm about to talk to my sister, goodnight," Farren told Chanel and left the room.

Chanel prayed that Farren didn't invite her sister to Miami, she just wanted them to spend some time together.

Farren went to check on her children before retreating to Chanel's guest room.

"Bitch, I'm going to fuck you up," Neeki shouted into the phone.

"I love you, I'm so sorry. Shit was real complicated," she told her sister.

"Are you okay?" she asked, concerned.

"I will be," she said honestly.

"I want to see you, how are the kids? Where y'all at?" she bombarded Farren with questions.

"I want you to meet my sister, can you come to Miami this weekend?" she asked.

"Sister?"

"Yeah, my daddy's other daughter, she cool. She's younger than us," she said.

"Hmm, okay honey, I'll come down Thursday night, I got a lil' boo there," Neeki said.

Farren wasn't going to tell Mario she pushed the trip back a few days, she was just going to show up and surprise him. Mario already thought she was full of shit anyway so Farren didn't see the need to call him with an excuse.

"Okay, sounds good," Farren told her sister.

"I love you," she said.

"Love you more," Farren told her.

Farren hated to think about what everyone went through once they found out that she was "dead". No one besides her children crossed her mind; they were the only ones that she was concerned with. Farren wanted to repair the hurt of so many hearts, but she knew that wasn't possible. In this "new life" she was done bending over backwards for people. Farren was only concerned with the well-being of her children and herself.

Farren climbed under the covers and got cozy. She was praying that she didn't toss or turn in her sleep tonight. Greg was now dead and couldn't come back to haunt her nightmares or try and kill her again. Farren was so angry that she couldn't gut his ass like a fish, it wasn't fair. Farren hoped that Christian was smiling down at her from Heaven but if Farren really knew her husband like she swore up and down to anybody that she did, she would know that if Christian Knight was still living, he would have wanted Farren to get her children and return to Dubai. Why would she try to return to The Roundtable? Farren didn't make sound decisions, she based everything off of emotion and soon she would learn that was the wrong thing to do.

When handling business with people, whether you fuck with them or not, never make a decision based off emotions. Think before you speak and before you sign your name on the dotted line. When you have your heart in it, sometimes that leads to destruction. If Farren were really business minded and focused on the task at hand, then she would be thankful that James came into the living room when he did and that he killed Greg's wife and wiped down the home with bleach. Farren was about to walk out of the house without removing any trace of her ever visiting the home just because she was caught up in the thought of Greg killing Christian Knight and attempting to kill her.

True enough, Farren had learned a lot from her father and Jeff, but she was still very rough around the edges and she made careless mistakes. If she thought the Cartel was about to vote her back in, she needed to do some more training because she was not equipped mentally to run a multi-billion dollar organization without ending up in the FFDS or dead for real this time.

Chapter 5

Farren opened the bathroom door and her sisters smacked their lips. She smiled already knowing why they were mad.

"What's wrong?" she was acting like she clueless.

"You said we weren't dressing up," Chanel whined.

"We're not," Farren laughed.

"Girl, that's Farren for you! Always gotta be the baddest bitch in the club," Neeki teased.

"Oh whatever, y'all heffas ready?" Farren said, adding a coat of her favorite MAC lip-gloss, Underage.

"I just need some perfume," Chanel said, standing and pulling down her dress that she snatched up from Bebe earlier when they went to the mall. She thought her outfit was cute until her big sister entered the room looking and smelling like a million bucks.

Farren was dressed in a white bandage dress and a graffiti inspired, cutout corset top from Valentino. The electric blue pumps with fringes had her calf muscles and toned, thick thighs looking good as hell. Farren never had any surgery and even after pushing four children out of her and breastfeeding all of them, her body still looked unharmed and untouched. Who got shot a few times and was in a medical-induced coma for five months, not Farren Knight. She looked breathtaking.

Her sister Nikita was dressed in True Religion jeans, Gucci sandals, and a white V-neck. She said she was too drunk and high to get dressed.

"Where are we going?" Chanel asked from the backseat of the Escalade truck.

She was definitely enjoying her first night in Miami, Florida. Farren's friend, Mario had them staying in one of his villas on the beach in Miami. They spent the first few hours after their private flight landed, soaking up the sun on the beach and drinking peach mojitos. Chanel had never had anyone wait on her hand and foot; it seemed like nothing new to Farren. Chanel's mouth was speechless when she saw how much money Farren was spending on clothes, food, and drinks. It was as if it was nothing to her. She never even counted the amount she handed the waitress.

Chanel had stopped her earlier. "You just tipped her like a hundred dollars," she said.

"That girl probably got three kids and ain't making nothing but seven dollars an hour, we good sis, no worries," she told her and went back to drinking her drink and pushing her feet further in the sand. Chanel wondered how much money did Farren really have. It had to be more than a few million, considering she was spending money like it was nothing to her. Chanel on the other hand, only came with a few thousand. When James asked her did she need anything, she quickly told him no. A man would never be able to feel like they did for her and she was obligated to love him because of what he provided for her. Chanel was Ms. Independent and she was keeping it that way for the rest of her life. She had learned a very valuable lesson in dealing with Quincy's crazy ass.

"Just sit back and ride sis, you wanna hit the blunt?" Neeki asked her. Chanel told her no, she was happy that her and Neeki had kicked it off. Neeki acted more like Chanel; it was safe to say that Farren Knight was in her own lane and had been her whole life.

Farren turned up the radio and did ninety on the highway, heading to one of her favorite clubs while she visited Miami, Florida.

"It's crowded as hell," Neeki said when they turned into the Fontainebleau entrance.

Farren remained quiet as she pulled up and left the truck with valet. She paid the security guard extra to let her enter the club with her gun. Even though Greg was dead, and she knew he was dead, her ass was still very paranoid and refused to ever be caught slipping.

An hour into partying at the club, Farren had ordered bottles and was standing on the couch singing and dancing with her sisters. An eerie feeling came over her, but she brushed it off.

The feeling returned ten minutes later. Farren got off the couch and sat down. Something was off...something wasn't right and she felt it. Chanel peeped the uneasiness on Farren's face. "What's wrong?" she asked.

"I feel like I'm being watched," Farren said in her ear. It was so loud in the club she could barely hear her thoughts. That wasn't a good thing, Farren needed to hear herself think.

Farren stood and peeped into the crowd, it was so dark and foggy.

That's when she saw him.

"What the fuck!" she said, pulling her gun out of her Chanel clutch and taking off into the crowd.

"Where is she going?" Neeki yelled over the music. Chanel shrugged her shoulders.

"I don't know but come on." She pulled her down from the couch and they left their private VIP section and struggled to keep up with Farren. Chanel didn't know how she managed to migrate through the crowded club in six-inch heels and to add to that, Farren had been drinking and smoking all day.

Farren was pissed off and didn't appreciate HIM being exactly where she was, less than a few feet away from her at that. She knew something wasn't right, she had felt it in the shower when she kept dropping the soap and had cut her legs trying to shave. Farren felt it when she was rolling a blunt and kept fucking up the weed. She felt it when she was applying her eyeliner and poked herself in the eye. Farren knew something wasn't right.

Why in the world did she think just because Greg had died, she would have peace? This Cartel shit was crazy and it was starting to get on her motherfucking nerves. Farren couldn't even enjoy a night out in hot ass Miami with her beautiful sisters, without having to pull her gun out.

She finally entered the section in which he was posted. What bothered her was that he was unfazed by her presence, but that was just how he was. He told her on numerous occasions, he didn't give a fuck who she was. None of that meant nothing to her; he was with her because he wanted to be. Her diamonds, furs, foreign cars with the pink slips, Chanel robes with the matching slippers, twenty thousand square feet condo in the Bahamas, didn't mean shit to him. He was with her because she could cook, roll a fat blunt, and her head was the bomb.com

He was unconcerned with her bank account and how she had the red bottoms before anyone else.

"Pull that gun out if you want to boo, you better kill me," he told her.

Chanel and Nikita finally came behind their sister.

"What are you doing here? You following me?" Farren asked.

He laughed and took a pull on his blunt, before pulling his Balmain jeans over his Burberry boxers.

His niggas were eyeing her and her thick ass sisters, not even knowing who the sexy Cougar was all in their man's face.

"Farren, you and I both know I'm not following you, for what?" he told her.

She rolled her eyes. His nonchalant attitude is what turned her off and turned her on at the same time.

"Fuck you," she said mushing him in the head before turning on her heels and walking off.

He grabbed her hand, and pulled her into him.

"Why you causing a scene?" he whispered in her ear.

Chanel didn't know whether to jump on his ass or bite his lip. He smelled good and looked even better.

"I'm not, just want to know what the fuck you doing in Miami?" she asked.

"Bianchi dead, ain't no point in me laying low. Time to get back to the money," he told her.

"Cool, well enjoy your night, be safe," she told him, walking off.

He called out to her. She turned around and he threw his iPhone at her.

"I'll call you later, pick up," he told her.

Farren waved him off but she did slide the phone in her purse.

"Are we leaving?" Chanel asked.

"Girl nah, we gotta turn up more now that I have an audience," she said.

They went back to their section. Farren had security remove the peasants who thought that those were free seats, but it was ten thousand to rope that section off and it was just Chanel, Neeki, and Farren in there turning up.

Farren bossed up and sent bottles and Cuban cigars to his section. He held a bottle up to signify cheers.

She held her glass up to him.

Who knows what the night had in store for Farren, she secretly hoped that when the sun came up, he had his head between her legs.

"Girl you is turnt," Neeki said laughing. Farren smiled at her sister. She wouldn't admit that seeing him had her in her feelings. She was having fun before she peeped him but she really was about to start having fun now.

Farren really enjoyed her night and so did Chanel and Neeki. Unbeknownst to Farren Knight, Mario had watched the whole situation unfold and couldn't believe that hood nigga was still living. Mario held Farren when she cried about losing all of her lovers; he wondered what else she had been lying about this whole time. His trust and patience was beginning to wear thin with little Miss Farren Knight.

"Y'all come on," Chanel complained, her dogs were barking. She was a three to four inch heel kind of girl and wore heels to meetings only. Other than that, around the office she had her comfortable flats on.

"We coming granny," Farren laughed.

She told her sister to drive; Farren was toasted.

They sung to the songs on the radio as they headed back to Mario's villa.

"Hold on, turn that down," Farren said.

"Hello," she answered his cell phone.

"Go get us a room at the Viceroy," he said into the phone.

"Okay," she said and hung the phone up.

"Girl, who the fuck is that?" Chanel asked.

"One of my old lovers," Farren said batting her eyelashes.

"Hmm, okay honey, be safe," Chanel said.

"Always, I have no problem killing me a motherfucker, trust and believe that," Farren said.

"Sis, you doing it like that?" Neeki asked.

Farren ignored her. Chanel noticed that Farren only discussed what she wanted to, she rarely answered or responded to anything someone would say to her.

"I'm hungry, let's do brunch in the morning," Farren suggested.

"Sounds good to me," Neeki said.

"What about you Chanel or is James popping up on you?" Farren teased.

"Girl I doubt it, he's mad because I wouldn't let him give me any shopping money," she told her.

"What you think we been spending this whole time? Your nigga's money, haan!" Farren burst out laughing.

Chanel sat her head in between the driver and passenger's seat. "For real? When did you see him?" she asked.

"He put it in my account. You better let that old rich ass nigga show you a few things honey, you playing," Farren said.

"I hear that sis," Neeki high-fived Farren.

"I don't want him thinking I need him," Chanel shook her head.

"And if he a real nigga, which he is, he already know you don't, so what's the issue?"

"I've had niggas take care of me I don't want that no more, it should be equal."

"What does equal mean?" Neeki asked.

"50/50 you do for me I do for you, I pay you pay," Chanel informed her.

Farren shook her head and said loudly, "Oh hell nah," she said.

She continued, "50/50? Girl and you fucking and sucking on this nigga, that alone is the 50. Let's not forget to add cleaning and cooking, putting up with his shit, shit, that's ten more percent. Nah boo boo, see my mama raised us on the 70/30, and thirty being a lot," Farren laughed.

Neeki shook her head in agreement.

"Are y'all serious?" Chanel asked, shocked.

"Girl what the fuck you mean? Hell yeah! I never, ever in my life dated a broke nigga. Even Jonte had money. He ain't have much as me, but he still spoiled the hell out of me," she said.

"And then you bought him that Rolls Royce for Christmas," Neeki added.

Chanel shouted, "A Rolls Royce? You bought a nigga a Rolls Royce?"

Farren said, "Yes, he deserved it, and plus I was tired of him riding around in that damn Audi, everybody knew his car. I think every man should have at LEAST three cars and hell, Chrissy had about eleven," Farren said.

"So you telling me you don't feel like a gold digger when you only date a man for his money?" Chanel asked.

Farren was drunk and she knew she was drunk so she tried her hardest not to go off on her sister. "First and foremost, my daddy had money so I never NEEDED a nigga for nothing, but honey, this pussy was never free, so call it what you want, I just wasn't dating a man who couldn't provide."

"And that's not called a gold digger to you?"

"Look, if you broke when you get to your nigga house and broke when you leave, then you a dumb ass. If your car was on half when you got to his house and on E when you got back home, that's your dumb ass," Farren said matter-of-factly.

Chanel didn't agree, but maybe it's because she realized that after Quincy died she depended on him for everything and she had nothing.

"I can never put my life into a nigga's hands," Chanel said.

"Who told you to?" Neeki asked.

"Always have your own baby girl," Farren told her.

"But you're spending your dead husband's money, you don't have your own," Chanel said.

Neeki stopped the car. Farren turned around, she smiled at Chanel.

Chanel's heart stopped; Farren looked evil as hell. What in the world was about to happen?

"You really don't know me," Farren told her.

Farren turned the radio back up and just like that, the conversation was over.

"I'll see y'all in the morning," she told her sisters and got out of the car. Neeki brought her to the lobby of the hotel so she could check into a room.

Neeki told Chanel, "Girl, get your ass in the front, I ain't driving no Miss Daisy," she said.

"Is she mad?" Chanel asked.

"Mad for what? You don't know what the hell you talking about cus if you did you wouldn't have said that," Neeki said nonchalantly. They both were just like their mother, nothing bothered them, they were so insensitive.

"But I see her spending money like it's nothing," she said.

"That's not your business though, what does that have to do with you?"

Chanel had nothing to say.

"You have a lot to learn about Farren and you better learn fast before she cuts your ass off," Neeki told her.

Chanel still had questions, she had a lot of questions and she needed answers. She didn't want everything that came out of her mouth to offend her sister, that's not what she wanted at all.

Farren checked in the room, and left a key for him at the counter but didn't text him any details until she had bathed and had a robe wrapped around her body. Farren ordered a steak from room service and was going through his phone.

She wasn't surprised at all to see him texting a plethora of bitches. He wasn't one to feed a woman lies. His conversation was pretty simple; what you doing, come over, what you cook and her all-time favorite, left money on the counter for you.

Just a like a hood nigga to not care about how a woman was feeling and how her day was. She had taught him better than that, but it seemed as if he didn't care about what he learned; he was just fucking and ducking these hoes.

After Neeki texted her saying they had made it to Mario's villa safely, Farren turned all the lights off and fell asleep. She was already drunk and high, sleep was about to be too good.

Click. Clack.

Farren assumed she was having another dream of a bullet coming at her, but oh no, it wasn't a dream, a gun was really being pointed at her temple.

She opened her eyes quickly, wondering what in the fuck was going on and who had gotten in her hotel room.

When she saw that it was him, her heartbeat decreased. He wouldn't kill her nor would he admit how much he really loved her, both were too complicated for him to do.

"That's how you greet me?" Farren asked, moving the gun out of her face.

"Wanted to make sure that pussy was extra wet," he said nonchalantly, tossing the gun on the nightstand.

"And you think a gun being pushed in the side of my head makes me cum?" she asked sarcastically.

"Yep," he said, removing his clothes and going for the shower.

Farren followed him to the bathroom, "Portia, Altese, Laronda oh, and some old looking bitch named Ethel all sent pics and goodnight text," she told him.

He ignored her and stepped into the shower.

"Did you hear me?" she asked.

"I'm sure you told them that I was unavailable," he shouted.

"No, I'm not your woman," she snapped.

"If you say so. Why are you watching me? Go roll me a blunt and order me something to eat, ain't they room service twenty-four hours?" he asked.

"Yes, what would you like sir?"

"You already know what I like to eat, did you forget?"

His mouth was off the chain. She would have to get used to this all over again. Farren did as he asked, and when he stepped out of the shower and wrapped up his conversation, there was a knock on the door with a late breakfast.

Farren watched him smoke and scarf down his food.

"When did you get back?"

"How did you know I wasn't dead?"

"I just knew... the funeral didn't feel right."

"You went?" she was surprised.

"Didn't stay long, I came before everybody got there," he told her.

"Hmm, did you cry?" she asked.

"Nah," he said.

"I missed you," Farren admitted.

"Then why did you shoot at me?" he asked.

She saw the anger in his eyes and told herself it was time to go. Anybody that greeted the woman they swore they loved with a gun to their temple, clearly had issues. Farren was about to dip. They could never progress if he was harboring ill feelings.

"I'm about to go, it was good seeing you Kool, take care," she told him, untying the robe and putting her clothes and jewelry back on.

"Where you going?" he asked.

"You secretly want to kill me; I can't stick around until you do that."

He chuckled, "Secretly? I don't have to do anything in secret bae, if I wanted to kill you I would have just done it. You know, like how you shot at me?"

"See, there you go again! Why we gotta keep going through this?" she fussed.

"Because you let that fat Italian fuck get in your mind man, you tried to fucking kill me. When your gun jammed, that's when you realized you were making a mistake, but then you fixed it and shot me anyway, like what the fuck?"

"But you lived, you fucking lived. I could have killed you. My aim is the shit buddd I don't miss."

Kool wiped his mouth and he walked up on her. Farren took a few steps back but he backed her up against the wall. He pulled another small gun from the back of his basketball shorts, and touched her lips with the gun.

"See how easy it is to kill you? Trust me, if I wanted to off you, I would have done it. I trust you so trust me," he told her.

Farren didn't believe shit he was saying and she wanted to exit that hotel room ASAP.

"Kool, I swear before God, if you don't get that gun out of my face…" she told him through clenched teeth.

"Or what?" he taunted, biting her cheek.

She pushed him off her and threw a lamp in his direction.

"Damn, that's how you do?" he asked.

"Fuck you," she told him turning around.

Kool snatched her up by her hair and pushed her back up against the wall. He attacked her mouth, kissing her so passionately and biting her bottom lip so hard, that he drew blood from it.

"Move," she moaned.

"Why?" he asked, licking and kissing all over her neck.

"I'm not fucking you," she told him.

"Good, cus I ain't need you to do nothing but lay here and let me put my dick in you," he told her, flinging her over his back and throwing her on the bed.

Farren wanted to protest but the truth was, she was horny and hadn't had sex in a year. Her pussy was feening to be penetrated and stroked.

Kool looked over at her body and her stomach was full of scars from her surgeries.

"What happened?" he asked, running his hands over all of the scars.

"People who worked on me ain't know what the fuck they were doing," she said, covering her stomach up.

"Stop," Kool told her removing her hands. He was amazed at the woman lying before him; she survived. Kool could only imagine all of that bullshit Farren had endured with struggling to survive.

"I salute you ma, these are war wounds," he told her. Kool leaned down and kissed every single scar on her stomach. He took his time whispering love affirmations in her ear. Kool wanted her to know that she was still the baddest bitch he ever laid eyes on and was the ONLY woman he ever spent money on and did shit for. Farren had that aura about herself, made a nigga empty his pockets when he came into her presence. Kool stepped his shit up once he got with Farren. She was one of those ladies that you considered a treasured gem, she was in rare form. Kool knew that he couldn't be mediocre when dealing with Farren Knight.

"Why did you let me live?" he asked.

Hours after, they spent time making love to each other.

"Kool," she whined his name.

"Nah man, for real, I think about that shit all the time."

"You didn't deserve to die."

"So you had no problem killing me if you had a reason to?" he asked.

Farren turned around and faced him. "If I feel like you cross me right now I will kill you."

"Just like that?" he was surprised. Farren was a little mean when he got with her, but now she was just downright ruthless.

"With no hesitation," she told him straight up.

"Sounds 'bout right boo," Kool told her, kissing her juicy lips and slipping his hand in between her legs. That pussy was so tight and sweet; he had to hit it one more time before she dipped.

"I'm sore," she told him closing her legs and turning around.

"I don't care, bend over," he told her, slapping her thigh.

Farren wanted to argue but she didn't, knowing good and damn well she wanted and needed more as well.

She got on all fours and placed her neck on the end of the pillow. Farren knew her pussy was already wet as fuck, but it didn't help to get it sloppier for Kool. She began toying with her clit, allowing Kool's dick to get hard off the wet sounds her pussy was producing.

"You ready ain't ya?" Kool teased.

"Mmm hmm," she moaned.

Farren closed her eyes as Kool entered her slowly.

"Damn that pussy still tight," he whispered.

Farren got comfortable on her elbows; she let him do his thing before she started throwing it back. She turned around to watch his lips curl up.

She loved to see a nigga try to control his facial emotions knowing good and damn well it was feeling too good to not nut up.

Farren licked her lips and winked her eye, but Kool couldn't keep looking at Farren, he would be nutting if he did.

She started twerking up and down on his dick.

"Damn baby," Kool said slapping her ass.

Farren turned around and wrapped her legs around his neck; she licked and pulled on her own brown, round nipples, while Kool stroked her middle real fast.

This was the perfect example of a morning quickie. Kool had Farren cumming back to back. Soon it ended and they both climaxed.

"Call down to the front desk and tell them we need another night, I'm not done tearing that pussy up," Kool told her, going to take a shower. His body was sticky from Farren's pussy squirting all over his stomach and chest.

She rolled her eyes but did as he asked, because she wanted more too. Farren texted her sisters and told them to enjoy their day and she would catch up later, before curling up with Kool and taking a nap.

They spent the day laying up, fucking, smoking, and sleeping.

"You living here or you back in Atlanta?" she asked.

"Neither, I been out in Charlotte getting a lil money, nothing like I'm used to," he admitted.

"You need a new plug?" she asked.

He handed her the blunt, "Nah, I need to go back to being the plug, I was making hella money before I got knocked," he told her.

"I'm on the outside right now."

"You not going back?" he asked.

"I've been thinking about it, I'm not sure," she admitted.

"They need you, I heard they ain't been making no money cus they product whack as fuck," Kool told her.

"Hmm, I haven't heard that," she said.

"Of course you not gon' hear it from them, ask some users, two thumbs down," Kool said.

Farren went and got in the bed. She didn't want to talk business, she needed another nap.

The next day, her and her sisters were laid out on the beach.

"You never told us how your night was?" Chanel asked.

"I don't kiss and tell," Farren told her seriously.

Chanel rolled her eyes, "It's called girl talk."

"If it ain't about the money no discussion needed," she told her younger sister. Chanel had so much to learn about life, friendships, sisterhood, and privacy. Farren and Christian Knight's marriage didn't last as long as it did off of loose lips. When Farren had a problem with her husband, she handled it with him; she didn't run and call her best friend or his mother.

It was years later before Farren started sharing her personal feelings towards Christian and how he had basically abandoned their marriage and their vows. Farren believed that what went on behind closed doors stayed behind closed doors. Half of the time, Christian and Farren would go days without talking, but to his family and even their business associates, they were the perfect couple.

When you begin to include people in your relationship that's when naysayers opinions become relevant, when their opinions should never matter. Farren learned her lesson a long time ago in dealing with a married man, Dice. Everyone and their mama had an opinion about Farren sleeping around with Dice, and it eventually changed the way she operated with Dice.

"Well did you at least enjoy yourself?" she asked.

"Yes I did, y'all wanna order another round?" Farren asked.

Neeki said, "Yasss bitch turn up."

Minutes later, "Cheers to love and happiness, oh, and making money," Farren said, and they all downed double shots of Patron.

"What we doing today?" Chanel asked.

"I'm chilling," Neeki said.

"Me too," Farren said.

Chanel decided to just lay back and relax. Come tomorrow she would be back to work anyway, might as well enjoy her free time while she could.

The weather was perfect and the water wasn't freezing cold. As long as the drinks kept coming along with the calamari and spring rolls, Chanel and the girls would be out here all day.

Mario walked down the beach to them. "Farren, looking good mama," he told her.

She didn't know what was cute about her today. She had on shades and a long summer dress, for two reasons. One, she hated her stomach and two, Kool left passion marks from her neck on down. Farren had marks behind her neck and ears, her titties, her arms, her thighs and all over her ass. That nigga fucked her all in the shower, the balcony; they tore that room up. Her pussy was so swollen she could barely walk, but she didn't care because she would be limping right back to his ass tonight before her plane took off.

"Thanks boo," Farren told him, smiling.

"What's up?" she asked. Farren had been around him long enough to know good and well when he wanted something.

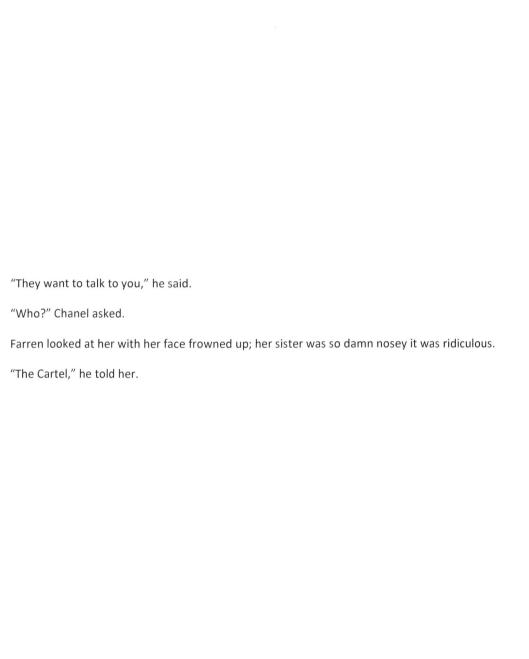

"They want to talk to you," he said.

"Who?" Chanel asked.

Farren looked at her with her face frowned up; her sister was so damn nosey it was ridiculous.

"The Cartel," he told her.

Chapter 6

"Are you sure you gone be straight going by yourself?" Chanel asked her big sister for the millionth time.

Farren chuckled, "Girl yes, Mario's family loves me, I'm good, I promise. Thank you though," Farren told her. She put her blunt out and went to stand, but a sharp pain made her sit back down. "Fuck," she grunted.

"You okay?" Neeki asked.

"My stomach keeps hurting," Farren mumbled. Chanel looked at her sister and she had tears in her eyes. She was in real pain, no lie.

Neeki got up from the couch and asked Chanel to help her lay Farren down on her back. Neeki lifted Farren's silk blouse and hissed at the bruises and barely sown up stitches and stuff.

"Farren what the fuck?" she said angrily.

"I'm okay, I promise," she told her sister.

"How long has it been like that?"

"Months," she said, out of breath.

"Girl, are you serious?" Neeki said, rushing to her cell phone to call an ambulance.

"Neeki no, don't call anyone, please, I'm okay. I just haven't been taking my pills," she struggled to get the words out.

"Then you been smoking, are you stupid?" Chanel fussed.

One hour later, Farren was admitted into the hospital and the doctors had decided to keep her.

"So I need surgery and how long does that take? I have a closing to get to for my new house, then my kids are in someone else's care," Farren fussed.

The doctors wasn't hearing shit she was saying. She had a lung that was seconds away from collapsing and Farren smoking all throughout the day, wasn't helping at all.

"Ma'am, get comfortable," the nurse told her and walked out of the room.

Farren called Mario and told them the meeting location had been moved from Ruth Chris to hospital room 2900.

She pulled out her infamous little black book, which was another one of the items Farren made Mario go get from the house.

"So what are we meeting about today?" Farren asked.

The head of one of the families looked over in Chanel and Neeki's direction, and wondered why they were present at the meeting.

"They're good," she said.

Still the few members that were present weren't comfortable with people who didn't belong to The Cartel listening to classified business.

"We will go get some lunch, call us if you need anything," Neeki said and Chanel followed. She stopped and kissed her sister's cheek and whispered, "Love you." in her ear.

Neeki smiled. Chanel was very open with her admiration for her big sister. She thought it was cute, especially since Neeki and Farren had never been like that before. It wasn't that they didn't love each other because they did, very much so. It was shown through actions not words, but that's just how they were raised. Neeki could count on one hand how many times Nakia had told them she loved them and she was proud of them.

"Okay what's up?" she said once the door was closed.

"First, it's good to see that you are alive and kicking."

"'Is it true that Greg has been taken care of?" one of the members asked.

Farren nodded but never offered a verbal response.

Someone said in Spanish, "You owe me a million dollars; I told you she handled it."

"Oh fuck off," he argued back.

"You do know that Bianchi was murdered a year ago and we have yet to discover his killer?" another member stated.

"Who gives a fuck?" Mario mumbled. Some rolled their eyes at the youngin's disrespect and others nodded their head silently agreeing.

Bianchi's death was bittersweet, although his funeral was the largest, even nobler than Christian Knight's. Many of the members of The Cartel only went to make sure that the fucker was dead for real. Bianchi had ended so many lives and made tons of poor business decisions based off emotions and petty arguments. Bianchi wasn't a fair leader at all and even after his death, The Cartel felt like they were still suffering as if he left a curse over The Cartel.

"Will you be at The Roundtable?" someone asked Farren.

"I doubt it," she lied.

"We believe that you should nominate yourself."

"I have lost too many of my loved ones to The Cartel, no thank you." Farren had to play everything cool.

"You have your father and your husband's spirit in you, you got this."

"I heard Kim is going around trying to gain votes," Mario said looking at Farren.

He knew good and damn well Farren hated Kim, which is the only reason he said something. Farren rolled her eyes at his childish antics.

"I will let you all know," Farren told them and thanked everyone for coming to see her.

"I prayed for you," one of the members told her before leaving the room. Farren flashed her million-dollar smile at him. He was always a sweetie pie.

Mario stayed behind as expected. Farren squeezed the button for morphine. Her body really needed it; her back was fucking killing her.

"How are you feeling?" he asked.

"Like shit," she admitted.

"You've been running around too much, all in the club standing on couches and shit," he said.

Farren moved her head out of his hold. "Excuse me?" she said.

"You should have stayed in Dubai, your body wasn't healed," he said.

"I was dying in Dubai and turning into a pill popping animal," she said with her face frowned up.

"At least you were safe," he told her.

"Mario, I need some sleep," Farren dismissed him.

"When were you going to tell me about him?"

"Mario, what was there to tell? That had nothing to do with you honestly," she told him.

"Nothing to do with me? You told me you had no one and you were alone, did you forget that shit? I'm the one who saw about you, not him!" he shouted.

She sat up in her hospital bed, pain running through her body and all.

"You need to get off that shit, it's making you crazy," she told him, genuinely concerned about his well-being.

"Farren you changed," Mario shook his head.

"Changed? Mario, what the fuck are you talking about? Man, get out, I already don't feel good. You're giving me a headache," she told him.

"You promised me that we would be together once your heart healed, but then you get a room with that pussy boy for two days straight. Where is he now, huh?" he yelled, knocking the medical tray over.

Farren had a gun behind her pillow, and restrained to this hospital bed and all, she had no problem shooting at his ass if he got out of control.

"I'm right here, what's up?" Kool asked him with his arms crossed, his gun was on full display and he wasn't trying to hide it with his Polo t-shirt.

His niggas were right behind him ready for whatever.

Mario could hold his own, he wasn't no weak man at all, but Kool was from the hood, Mario was born into a wealthy family. Farren didn't knock anybody on how they were raised, but she was a firm believer that people from the hood could fight better than anybody else. Farren grew up fighting her cousins, niggas and their bitches, dogs and all.

"You get some rest Farren and call me next week," Mario told Farren and bypassed them.

"Baby, you good?" Kool planted a wet kiss on her lips. She started moaning not giving a fuck that his friends and her sisters were in the room.

"Chill out ma," he told her, laughing.

"Honey, when he comes around you actually smile," Chanel joked.

Farren flipped her middle finger.

"He is so creepy to me, I been told you that," Neeki told her sister.

"I told you he be on that wet, he gotta stop fucking with them drugs," she said.

"How long you gon' be in here?" Kool asked.

"Man, I don't know. I'm trying to see if they can transfer me to Emory, I gotta get to my kids," she said.

"Who we need to talk to?" he asked.

"My sister gone handle it, she's a nurse," she told him. Kool seemed concerned about Farren and she appreciated that for real.

"What time you heading back?" she asked him.

"Now, I was just coming to make sure you was straight, it look like I came right on time," he said.

"I'll see you soon," she told him.

"Fa sho," he told her.

"You not going to introduce us to your friend?" Chanel asked.

"This is Kool my friend, my sisters Neeki and Chanel," she introduced them. Kool only nodded, he wasn't one for a lot of attention. Actually, no one Farren had ever talked to was. She preferred a low-key man anyway.

"What it do?" he said.

Farren blushed. Kool was so sexy to her and he wasn't one of those niggas that just knew they were drop dead gorgeous. His mind was on money and that was all he cared about, bitches came and went in his book.

"Hand me that bag," Farren told Neeki. She threw her a MCM book bag.

Farren zipped the bag open, peeped into it and closed it back up before handing the book bag to Kool.

"What's this?" he asked.

"An 'I'm sorry' gift," she said winking her eye.

Kool opened the bag, and nodded his head. "I can dig it, fa sho," he said.

Farren smiled.

"We about to be out, be safe. I'll hit you when I land," he told her, kissing her forehead. When him and his homies left, Chanel whispered, "It was drugs in that bag?"

Farren laughed, "Girl you so green, hell nah, how he gone get on the plane with drugs?"

"What was in there then?"

"Money," she said.

"Now you were just preaching about not dating a broke nigga."

Farren rolled her eyes. "He's not broke and you don't understand and I don't feel like explaining it to you," she told her sister.

Farren laid back down in her hospital bed and closed her eyes, hoping that Chanel got the hint that the conversation was over. Farren felt bad about how things went down with Kool. She took him out of the game and cut his hustle off. Kool was one hard working ass nigga and the small amount of money she gave him should be able to help him get ahead, instead of hustling to pay rather than living. Half of Farren wondered was it really a coincidence that they were both in the club the same night, or was he lying and had been following her this whole time. Luckily, Neeki was able to convince the hospital to release her with the promise that she would be admitted into Piedmont Hospital upon returning to Atlanta, Georgia.

"You want to go straight to the hospital or go see the kids first?" Chanel asked, after they landed.

"Girl, fuck that hospital, take me to my babies. I got a busy week ahead of me," Farren said.

"You are going to go back to the doctor though right?" Chanel asked to make sure.

Farren nodded but she knew she wasn't going to the doctor; she had too much going on. Farren had to move into her home, decorate and go buy cars. It was time for her to get her kids back on track and back in all of their activities that they loved so much.

Farren yawned as soon as the garage door came down. "Girl, that plane got me tired as hell," Farren complained.

"Me too, but I need to iron and get ready for an 8 o'clock appointment," Chanel said.

"I remember them days," Farren told her as they walked into the house.

Chanel told her sister, "Girl, get out my way, I gotta pee," she fussed.

Farren turned around and looked at her little sister.

Chanel dropped her cell phone, she couldn't move. Farren went over to Chanel's grandmother's body, kneeled down and checked for any wounds or anything out of the normal. Her heart wasn't beating. She prayed to God that this lady died of natural causes and not anything related to Farren's bullshit with The Cartel. Her heart went out to her children and she took off to the room that they were sleeping in. Farren hated to leave Chanel in there by herself, but she had to make sure her kids were good.

They were knocked out, sleeping and slobbing like the little perfect angels they were. Farren's heartbeat slowed down when she saw they were okay. She kissed each of them before closing the door and going back to the kitchen.

"I'm assuming she had a heart attack or something. The floor isn't wet so she couldn't have slipped," Chanel mumbled.

"I will call the ambulance so they can come get her to do a full exam," Farren told her.

"No," Chanel cried.

"They have to come get her now before too much time passes, if you're going to donate her organs," Farren told her.

"Organs? That's what's on your mind? Saving someone else's life? Get the fuck out of my face," Chanel told her.

"Excuse me?" Farren said.

"My grandmother is dead. The woman who raised me is on my kitchen floor fucking dead, is everything business with you?" she yelled.

"Girl goodnight," Farren told her and walked off.

Chanel was happy that Farren walked off when she did because she was going through it and hated to have to swing on her older sister just because she was in her feelings. Chanel got up and grabbed the throw off the couch and went and laid down beside her grandmother on the hardwood floor. She cried herself to sleep, laying on her grandmother' chest.

Farren smoked so much that night because there was nothing else to do. She didn't want to be rude and ask Chanel for the keys to her car in the middle of her mourning her grandmother's death. She knew she had no business smoking, but she needed something to calm her nerves. Farren wanted to cry and be sad with her, but so many deaths back to back had her heart cold and she couldn't really relate anymore. Farren brainwashed herself to think that people died every single day and God didn't intend for anyone to be on earth forever. Farren felt like she had been through it all and nothing else could break her. She called her mother because she knew that she was up and probably wasn't doing anything but sitting in her window being nosey.

"Hey girl, what you doing?" Farren whispered into the phone.

"Why you whispering?" her mother asked.

"Chanel's grandma died, she in there crying so I don't want to be rude, all loud on the phone."

"Why you not in there with her?" her mom asked.

"Nobody was with me when Jonte died or when Ashley died or Christian or Carren, oh, and let me not forget Dice," Farren snapped.

"Farren, are you serious right now? Girl, please, you act like you the only one missing them or sad they died."

"Next subject," she said hastily.

"Well you called me heffa don't catch no attitude with me," she told her daughter.

"Ma, why did you go back to Hardy?" Farren asked out of nowhere.

Her mother was quiet on the other end of the line. Farren said "hello" to make sure she was still on the phone.

"Yeah I'm here," she said.

"Why didn't you and Daddy get married?" she asked another question.

"I wasn't everything he was looking for. I had some of the qualities, but not all of them," she said quietly.

"What does that even mean?"

"I wasn't pretty enough."

"Ma, don't say that," she said sadly.

"It's true, but I don't care anymore, and you only rubbed it in my face when you would come back home with y'all family pictures and stuff, talking about how much you love you some Diane. Diane this, Diane that. Girl I used to want to wring ya damn neck," she said.

Farren felt so bad now.

"Ma..."

"I'm good, your daddy dead now hell, don't none of us got 'em," she said coldly. A lump formed in Farren's throat and she didn't know what to say. Farren then prayed that she didn't become as cold as her mother or harbor ill feelings for years. Her mother had a serious chip on her shoulder.

"Will you be at the Roundtable?" she changed the subject.

"Still thinking about it, what you think?"

"Not sure yet, I'll let you know," her mother told her and hung the phone up. Farren had gotten used to her mother unplugging from her without warning, so she was officially unbothered.

Farren held herself tight. She wanted love she just didn't want to admit that she was lonely. Farren felt butterflies when she was in Kool's presence. She didn't experience the mushy feeling when she was with Mario, no matter how hard they both tried to create the feelings, they just didn't exist. Farren couldn't fake with no nigga, she didn't even see how her sister, who was very gay, had sex with men knowing a man couldn't satisfy her like a woman could. Farren didn't believe in faking with anyone, she was a very picky woman. She didn't date men with a sense of humor, it might sound crazy, but it was very much true. Men who laughed a lot or always found something funny when time was money, oh nah, Farren wouldn't give them the time of day. She didn't believe in talking to men who had messed up teeth. If she had to roll over and wake up to a man with a raggedy grill, she couldn't hide the dissatisfaction on her face; her facial expressions were always the worst. Farren couldn't date a man with kids, to each its own, but she didn't believe in playing stepmother or dealing with baby mama drama. Farren didn't believe in dating men who hated their mothers. Her question always remained "How can you love me if you don't respect the number one woman in your life?"

Farren believed in morals and standards, she couldn't settle or compromise her "list" for anyone, because men damn sure didn't compromise for women. If women actually thought about it, men were picky and they were very particular about what they were looking for. Now every so often you would find a man that loved every color of the rainbow, but for the most part, there were some men who preferred them a red bone and others who loved them a big bar of chocolate. Farren was thick, she had one or two back rolls and some stretch marks, she passed gas in her sleep, and snored when she was tired. She wasn't perfect and she never ever tried to be. Farren was a woman who just tried to be better than the person she was the day before. She was bossy, sometimes rude and standoffish, but her heart was made of gold. She was a lender and not a borrower and she had no problem closing her eyes and praying for you if need be.

With love and affection and all that other good shit on her mind, she called Kool.

"Speak," he said.

"Don't be telling me to speak."

"Hey man, I need to get my phone from you too," he said, instantly picking up on her voice.

"I'll mail it to you," she told him.

"Nah, I'll be that way in a few days, it's my mama's birthday," he told her.

"Hmm, okay," she said.

"What's that mean?" he asked.

"Nothing at all sir," she replied.

"Miss me?" he asked. Kool hated that he had let Farren back in so soon. She was supposed to suffer; he wanted her to sweat. He really wanted to kill her motherfucking ass, but he knew he didn't have the heart to do it. Farren had him wrapped around her finger and his tongue out his mouth like he was her lost puppy.

"I do."

"How much?" he asked.

"A lot."

"I miss you too shawty."

"How have your kids been?" he asked. Farren was surprised because that was the first time he had ever asked about her children.

"Well, they're getting used to mommy being back around."

"Fa sho, fa sho."

"Did you handle everything you needed to?" she asked.

"It's in the works," he said speaking in code.

"Let me know if you need something, there is a closet full."

"Word?" he asked.

"Yes."

"Why do you trust me?" he asked.

"Is there a reason why I shouldn't?" she asked back.

"Nah, just asking."

"Alright then."

"I don't like handouts," he said.

"Damn nigga, forget I said anything."

"Nah, like, I'm just saying, you be playing mind games."

"Call me when you get here," she brushed him off.

"We gotta discuss that shit man," he told her.

"It won't be tonight," Farren told him hanging the phone up. Niggas were always in their damn feelings. She didn't have time for the bullshit. Farren popped a Valium and took her ass to sleep.

The next morning, the children were all in the living room when Farren walked in. Noel came up to her mom and whispered ,"Madison crying about her big mama, she dead."

"I know baby, are you okay?" Farren asked.

Noel looked at her, "Yeah, she wasn't my grama."

Farren shook her head, her children had been through too much, but they were entirely too young to not have any emotions. Farren went and knocked on her sister's door.

"Hey, I'm going to give you and Madison some time, me and the kids going to look at cars and stuff," she said.

Chanel didn't say anything.

"Chanel, everything is going to be okay," Farren added.

"How can you say that? She was all I had."

"I've been where you are, everything will be okay, just pray. Do you want me to handle the funeral for you, I can basically plan them with my eyes closed?"

"I don't need your money," Chanel spat.

Farren was taken aback by her rudeness. She knew she was going through it so that's the only reason why she wasn't about to check her ass.

"Well that's good to know boo, but I was saying contact the church, get the coffin and dress," she told her.

"You don't know what my grandmother likes to wear," she went back and forth with Farren.

"Okay bitch, do it yourself I tried, text me the funeral arrangements," she said and prepared to walk out of her bedroom.

"You're so coldhearted."

"This is my last time telling you this, you don't know me okay, you don't know me at all. Until you have walked a mile in my shoes, please stop telling me who I am," Farren clapped her hands together as she said every single word. Her lil' sister was really about to see another side of her and it wouldn't be pretty.

The average woman, including her sister, Chanel Cavett, wouldn't be able to endure HALF of the shit that Farren had been through. She ain't want to hear nothing Chanel was saying about being coldhearted; coldhearted her ass. Farren hadn't shown her coldhearted at all.

The remainder of her day was spent breaking the mall down for her children and purchasing two cars.

"Do y'all like the new house?" she asked the kids as they sat at dinner.

"It needs some paint and curtains," Noel said.

"Well duh, mama ain't hooked it up yet," Michael told her.

"Can my room be black?" Morgan asked.

"Black?" Farren asked.

"Yes," she said.

"No, what about pink and white polka dots?"

"Mama, I want polka dots in my room," Noel said jealous.

"Okay baby. Morgan, what about something bright and fun?"

"Black," she shook her head and plopped a fry in her mouth.

Farren wondered what the dark colors were about. She really needed to stop playing and go take her kids to go see a psychiatrist.

"Can we go see daddy?"

"In New York?" Farren asked her son.

"Yeah, I just want to put some flowers on his grave," he said.

"Auntie Chloe used to take us like every day," Noel said.

"Okay pumpkins," she said. Anything her kids asked for, they would get. Her children had been through entirely too much. Once Ashley died, she really thought they were going to lose it. They had spent summers with Farren's best friend ever since they were little babies.

"What if we leave right now?" Farren asked.

"You bought the plane tickets already?" Noel asked surprised.

"Nope, but mommy can make things happen cus I'm supermom," Farren laughed. The only child that laughed was Morgan. Farren figured that Noel and Michael were getting too old for her corny jokes.

"Let's go." Farren left money on the table and slid out of the booth, with Morgan in tow.

"Mommy, do you miss working every day?" Noel asked, as they drove to the airport in an Uber.

"No, well... sometimes I do, but I get to spend more time with y'all."

"I miss Jonte," Noel said.

"My daddy?" Morgan asked.

"He was my daddy too," Noel said.

"Mine too," Farren whispered. She missed Jonte and she felt so bad every single day that he had to die because of the bullshit that he warned her about on so many different occasions.

With the children reminiscing about memories made with Jonte, Farren told herself she had to make sure Kim's ass was handled ASAP. She didn't know it, but her days were numbered.

But little did Farren know, Kim was already on her ass like white on rice. She was just waiting to go toe to toe with her. See, Farren was oblivious of how much Kim had played the game to get close to her, but she would soon find out that looks could be deceiving and everyone who smiles in your face does not always have your best interest at heart.

Farren wasn't warned about the wives and even the female workers in the Cartel. She didn't really fuck with any of them BUT Kim, and if she was smart, that would have been the one hoe she stayed far away from. Kim was a slut, a business-minded slut, because anybody she laid down with she was waking up the next morning with some information on them or the location to where they did they drop offs or something; she was by far not a dummy. Kim knew that Farren was beneficial; Kim knew that Farren's parents were the original members and they held a lot of power. Kim and Christian had them some fun back in the day until Farren shut that shit down. Until this day, Farren didn't know who was in his bed that night at the condo about twenty years ago.

"Shhh," Christian threw his hands over her mouth.

She was still fingering herself trying to catch her nut.

"I said shut the fuck up," he told her. The fear in his eyes shut her ass up real quick.

He had climbed out of bed and threw on his silk boxers that had been tossed over the chaise that was placed in front of the sleigh bed.

He picked up his gun on the dresser. When he walked into the kitchen, what he saw damn sure surprised him.

"Baby what you doing here?" he asked nervously.

"Well I was headed to a meeting when the receptionist called and said that there was a car parked in our spot and she was about to get it towed, but she was calling to make sure we didn't have any guests, because there are always cars parking in MY spot," Farren said never turning around from sipping her coffee at the breakfast bar.

Farren continued. "What day did you get back from your business trip, or did you even go out of town?" she asked.

"Farren," he pleaded.

She sat her coffee down and turned around to face her lying, cheating ass husband.

"Do you notice something different with me Christian?" she asked.

He shook his head.

"I'm not crying," she stated.

"What the fuck does that mean?"

"The old me would have went in there and beat that bitch's ass for being wrapped up in eight-hundred count sheets, knowing good and damn well you are a married man," she said above a whisper.

Farren was too playa to give a bitch the pleasure of knowing she pulled her out of character, but Christian was getting very lazy with his infidelities.

"Farren, it's not what you think."

"Tell me what do I think? I been sitting here listening to you make sweet love to some hoe, damn, you don't even last that long with me!" she threw a cheap shot.

"I love you Farren so let's not start please," he told her.

"Christian fuck you, wash the sheets before you leave," she told him and got off the bar and exited the condo just as quietly as she came.

When Christian returned to the bed, Kim was already getting dressed.

"I guess we're done for today," she said.

"Yeah, I need to get home," he mumbled.

"It was fun as always, see you next time," she told him, sliding her heels back on.

Christian never bothered to respond, he went straight to the shower.

Kim took the elevator to the main lobby and before going through the back door to get to her car, she slid the receptionist a hundred dollar bill for making that call. Christian Knight would be hers one day.

Chapter 7

"Farren, somebody is at the door for you!" Chanel told her sister. Farren was too busy flipping hot dogs and chicken wings on the grill.

Her new house was amazing and she was having a little, "Hey, I'm not dead" housewarming for a few close friends. Everybody was happy to see her smiling after so many deaths, and her day had been going well. Her children couldn't stay out of the pool for more than an hour, and she was delighted that each child got at least one thing that they requested in their new home. Farren rubbed her barbeque stained hands on her apron, before putting down the tongs to go see who was at the door. She looked around her backyard and saw that everyone who she had extended an invitation to had shown up, besides her sister who couldn't be away from work this weekend, because her business partner had already requested the weekend off.

Farren skipped through the home. She hadn't skipped since she was a little girl, but she was in a really good mood. It was something about God answering all of your prayers and showing up and showing out in your life, it placed a smile on your face that no devil in hell could erase.

Farren opened the door and the person at the door damn near caused her to have a stroke. What in the FUCK was HE doing at her door?

"Dice?" she asked.

"You gone let me in or what?" he asked, with a big smile on his face.

BEEP. BEEP. BEEP. BEEP.

Farren's alarm went off, waking her up from her sleep. The first thing she did was grab her gun, and hop out of the bed. Farren got up, locked her bedroom door, and peeped out of the window; there was no car in the driveway. She rambled around the bed for the damn remote to view the cameras she had around the house. She pressed "system" on the remote twice, which took it to the cameras. She was only able to peep one camera before whoever was in her house blacked that one out too.

Whoever was in her house had planned this shit, but whoever it was, better pray to God they killed her because she was one fed up bitch, and Farren was prepared for war. She cracked her neck and kicked her leg in the air.

"Come on bitches," she said, lighting a blunt. Farren didn't fear anything in life anymore; the only thing she was grateful about was that her children were not at home tonight, they were at Kennedy's house. Farren started to call James, but she told herself the police would be there soon, the alarm went off. Farren decided to kill whoever it was in her house and tell the police it was a robbery. She slid on some Timberlands that she had just copped, and what was ironic is that Farren just bought those boots today. She was taking her time trying to put her closet back together, since everything was basically taken from her. Farren opened her bedroom door and it was as if God was on her side, some dumb ass nigga had his back to her and she shot him down quickly. Farren only used guns with silencer.

Now the only thing she had to figure out was how many people was in her house.

"Find that hoe, why is this house so big?" she heard a woman say.

"Whose voice was that? Why did the voice sound so familiar?" she asked herself. Farren was racking her brain.

"Where is Tony?" the voice spoke again.

Farren moved closer to where she heard the voices coming from. It seemed as if they were on the lower floor. Farren peeped over the balcony, she was standing in the perfect position to take one of the people off their feet, and that's what she did.

Farren heard heels approaching the body and she stepped back so they couldn't see her. The woman kneeled down over one of her workers and turned around to see where the bullet could have come from.

She thought to herself, *This bitch has perfect aim.*

She looked up and saw Farren smiling dead at her ass.

But before she spoke, she shot her in her arm but not before Farren shot back twice. Kim fell on to her feet.

"Bitch," she yelled out.

Farren ran down the steps and shot at her again, but unlike Greg, Kim wouldn't be dying so soon.

Farren stood over her body, "Does it hurt?" she asked.

Kim said nothing, she grunted in pain. Farren kicked the gun out of her reach.

"How many people are in my house?"

"Bitch fuck you."

"I will feed you to my son's snake, how many people are in my house?" she pointed her gun at her.

"That's it."

"Driver?"

"I drove," Kim told her.

"Are you lying?" Farren asked. Kim looked at her; this bitch had loose screws in her head. Kim was able to see the long scar across her forehead that Farren normally hid with her hair and concealer throughout the day, but her hair was wrapped up.

"Kill me," Kim whined.

"No, I want to fuck you literally," Farren laughed.

She dragged her to the kitchen.

"Now the police are on the way, are you going to be a good girl while I talk to them?" Farren asked.

Kim was going in and out consciousness.

Farren slapped her, "Oh no bitch, you woke me up out of my good ass dream, we about to be up all night. You need some coffee?" Farren asked.

The doorbell chimed.

"Hold on honey, I have someone at the door," Farren told Kim.

"Coming!" she yelled.

Farren dragged Kim to the closet and locked the door. "Hope you don't die in here."

Farren opened the door. "I'm glad nobody was in here trying to kill me as long as y'all took," she said.

"Ma'am, the alarm company notified us, is everything okay?" the police officer asked.

"Yes I'm fine. I opened the garage door to get my charger out of the car and didn't get to the alarm in time. I called Comcast back but got impatient with being transferred to the security department," Farren said.

Of course, the police officers believed her. For goodness sake, Farren was one of the top attorneys in New York; she could sell crack to a person who was clean for thirty years, if need be.

Farren locked the door behind her and went to make sure all of the niggas in her house were dead and not just barely holding on. Farren didn't need anyone coming up behind her chopping her head off. She had learned a valuable lesson in escaping death; always make sure the heart ain't beating, not just slow.

Farren shot at the top of the closet and the bottom to see if Kim would yell, but she didn't. Farren opened the closet and she was in there, probably dead.

Farren threw some water on her and nothing happened, she dragged her out and opened her eyes but it was proven that she was gone.

Farren called James not knowing who else to call; this is what he did for a living in his past life. She went to open the door and Chanel was right behind him. Farren was disappointed.

"You bring your girlfriend when you're doing house calls?"

"I didn't know you were paying me," he said sarcastically.

"Farren, it's five in the morning, this couldn't wait?" Chanel complained.

"Would you be able to sleep if you had dead bodies all over your house?" she asked seriously.

"Dead bodies? James, that is not what you said," she fussed.

"Shut the fuck up!" Farren yelled.

Chanel looked at her, and James said nothing, because he was thinking the same thing.

He walked off and Farren followed him into the kitchen.

"I can't believe you killed her, this is going to be a problem," he said.

"I don't care she killed my baby daddy for no reason."

"That's why you killed her?" he asked.

"Uh yeah, why else would I?" she asked him, confused.

James snatched her shirt off, "For this," he said and big as day were the initials C.K.

Farren looked closer. "And that stands for what? Calvin Klein?" she asked.

James smirked. "Go take a bath, you're covered in blood and bring me your clothes," he told her.

Farren shook her head; she was even more pissed now that she wasn't able to kill the bitch how she wanted too. Farren was so sick of Christian Knight, and even from his grave, he was still bringing her problems. She would have never thought in a million years that Kim was secretly in love with Christian Knight. Farren knew she had did her lil' dirt growing up fooling with Dice, but one thing Dice didn't do, was parade his wife around. Christian never, ever, ever hid Farren Knight; she was not a secret at all.

Christian Knight loved his wife and told everyone he knew that Farren made him a better man. As much as Farren thought she was empty without him, Christian felt just as lost without his better half.

Farren let the water cascade down her naked body; she was filled with so much emotion. It had been so long since she cried and wept. She let it all out in the tub. Farren didn't care that her hair was getting wet even though she had been in the salon all morning. Farren watched the blood of Kim's trifling ass go down the drain and it did nothing to make her feel better. Farren thought the weight would be lifted from her shoulders, but she only felt heavier. This life, this dark demonic lifestyle, would be a part of her forever.

Farren had to get her kids from the bullshit; she didn't want any generational curses affecting them. Farren was angry, she was hurt, she was empty and alone and she didn't like that feeling. When did killing people become therapy, when did the need to have cameras and guns planted all over the house where her children played and laid their head at become her life?

Farren wondered what she was doing wrong because Christian Knight didn't have these problems, he didn't go through this shit. Drama never came to their front door. Farren didn't check over her shoulder when she was known as The Connect's Wife, but why?

And that's when it hit Farren like a lightning bolt. BECAUSE NOBODY FUCKING KNEW WHO SHE WAS!!!!!!!!!!!!!!!

Duh Farren! She banged her head on the wall of the shower; she called herself a big dummy.

Farren became the face of the Cartel, she was on hella flights, she was back and forth across the world. Farren didn't miss a meeting; she was at funerals and even weddings. Farren was active in the Cartel.

Farren took her time bathing and cleaning her body, because she was now doing some serious thinking. Christian never really went anywhere, he had a real job and he actually loved his job.

Christian didn't have drugs in their home, she wasn't even sure if he carried gun.

Christian never stressed out as much as Farren did.

Christian didn't argue or beef with niggas.

Farren had to switch it up but was it too late?

She dried off and threw on a matching pajama set. She felt a strong pain run through her body and told herself she really needed to go to the doctor.

Farren took the steps to the living room, looking for James. Chanel was in there knocked out, and Farren rolled her eyes. Lord knows she was so grateful for her lil' sister, but the girl had so much growing up and learning to do. Chanel didn't act like she was from the hood at all, she reminded Farren of a dumb blonde and it annoyed her so much.

It was as if Chanel forgot where she came from, and Farren didn't like that. Farren kept telling herself you will always need God and don't ever think all of this shit can't be taken from you in a matter of one second baby girl, because it can. "Stay humble" is what she told her sister every time she saw her.

Farren saw James in the garage rolling the bodies up in carpet.

"I just...ordered those rugs from Persia," Farren said with her lip curled. She had spent a grip on those rugs and couldn't wait until her furniture came in for her all white dining room.

"You can get some new ones, they were ugly if you ask me," he said.

"Can I ask you a question?" she asked, leaning on the hood of her car.

"Shoot," James told her, keeping his attention on the task at hand.

"What made Christian Knight, Christian Knight?" she asked.

James stopped what he was doing and took his gloves off.

"No lie, it ain't been a nigga like him in The Cartel yet. I don't give a damn what none of them say," James said.

"For real?" Farren said, surprised. She thought Mario handled his business well and plus he made his family and The Cartel a lot of money.

"Mannnn what? They all hated him. He was so smooth," James said.

"Boss man, you don't look nervous at all about this meeting," James said concerned. Not only was Christian Knight the man that signed his checks, but over the years he had grown extremely fond of the man he worked for.

"Nervous? Nah, they won't ever catch me breaking a sweat," Christian said calmly.

He fixed the tie on his Italian suit. Christian had been in meetings all day and was headed to the last one of the night, the illegal one, is what he liked to call it. Christian would choose his legal life over The Cartel bullshit any day. Why he chose this demonic lifestyle, he would never know. Tired of struggling, tired of not ever having enough, Christian hated that he let one person get him off track and make him lose sight of his goals, his goals of being a good Christian man and husband one day. His roommate in college introduced him to the game and Christian Knight ain't been the same since.

Christian appreciated the good ole days. Gone were the loyal men and women who did what was expected of them. The Cartel had changed and not for the good. Christian knew his time was coming; either death or jail, it was one or the other, but until either one of those motherfuckers knocked at his door, Christian Knight was here to stay. No man, no matter the amount in his bank account, the bitches in his stable or even how pure his coke was going to run Christian Knight up and out of his seat at The Roundtable. He had rightfully earned his position and worked damn hard to be where he was. Some couldn't even give him the credit he deserved, but he stopped looking for an applause a long time ago.

Farren asked, "He never wanted his own thing, like why didn't he just leave?"

"Start his own for what? Now don't get me wrong, I probably hate The Cartel way more than you do, but that shit had its perks, the benefits were endless, it was definitely worth the bullshit," he said.

"What you mean?" she asked.

James took a deep breath. He was sure that he knew way more about Christian Knight than Farren did.

"Nothing," James said, shook his head, and went back to wrapping up the dead bodies.

"James I have to get some kind of understanding on what's going on before I make my next move! It has to be my best move," she pleaded.

"And how does finding out about Christian's dirty dark secrets help?"

"I need to hear his voice."

"Farren, are you high or something?" he asked.

"Hell no, I'm just saying like why didn't he leave...what did they have over him for him to not leave?" she asked.

James remained silent.

"Why did they really kill my daughter?" she asked quietly.

James dropped the bungee rope.

Farren looked up and saw the look in his eyes.

"You know?" she asked. *He knows,* she thought to herself.

"But why? What happened? James, oh my, please tell me," she begged.

"You will never forgive him if you knew."

"He's dead," she said.

"Yeah but still," he shook his head.

"Was it his fault?" she asked.

Farren continued to dig for answers. "Just shake your head yes or no, that's the least you can do."

"Farren drop it," he told her.

"Okay, if you were me, would you leave The Cartel?" she asked.

James thought about it for a second, you could tell he was in deep thought; it was all over his face.

"Yeah...he never wanted this for you," he told her honestly.

"Well what did he want, shit," she snapped.

"Happiness. The Cartel is depressing, trust me, I'm still suffering," he told her.

"I was happy with Chrissy," she told James.

"But were you happy with Christian Knight?" he flipped the question which caused Farren to think.

Was I happy with Christian Knight? She thought to herself.

Hell, was I happy with FARREN KNIGHT. Farren closed her eyes and thought back to the good ole days or was she brainwashing herself to think they had happy days. No! No! No! They were a happy couple it was when that stupid stripper bitch, Asia came along...that's when all hell broke loose. Christian loved Farren, he really did.

She always knew when he was secretly stressing about something, it was in the way they had sex.

"Hmm... Yes... Ohh, ohhh...okay baby... okay baby...damn Chrissy you about to bite my shit off," Farren pushed her husband's head from in between her legs. He was being entirely too rough.

Christian ignored her, wiping her cum from his lips. He flipped her over and stuck his dick right into her with no warning. Although Farren was dripping wet, he still didn't have to be so forceful.

"Christian!" she moaned in anger and in pleasure.

"Shut the fuck up and take this dick!" he yelled, laying his hand in the crook of her back and pushing himself into her deeper.

They didn't connect at all during the sex and Farren counted down the seconds until it was over, she had tears in her eyes that he didn't even know had fallen.

Finally.

He climaxed all over her ass and rolled over without even bothering to go get her a warm washcloth as he normally did. Farren limped to the bathroom to take a quick and quiet shower, today was too much on her body. First a two-mile run this morning, then court all day in six-inch heels, the park with her children, one-hour spinning class, and she still made it home in a decent time frame to have dinner ready for her family. Mrs. Knight was one tired woman, but as always being the perfect wife she was, when her husband woke her up at four or five in the morning, after being God knows where all night demanding to lick her pussy, she opened her legs and gave him his heart desires.

Christian's eyes were bloodshot red and his breath reeked of alcohol, but Farren still made sure he nutted at least three times.

In the shower she told herself she couldn't continue to allow him to treat her like this. Too scared to ask anyone was this considered physical abuse, she just sucked it up and bathed and rinsed her body before getting out the shower. She oiled and lotioned her body down and slipped back into bed naked as the day she was born.

Christian rubbed her back, but she jumped at his touch.

Who wanted to fear their husband? She only felt this way when he came home with the world on his shoulders.

"What would you do if I told you I wanted us to move?"

"I would say okay," she told him honestly. Christian Knight could tell Farren they were going to the moon and her ass would have the kids' stuff packed up in a matter of ten minutes. Years into the marriage and three bigheaded kids later, she still was madly in love and head over for heels for her husband, the notorious Christian Knight

"Let's just go...to London or Dubai or Bora Bora."

"We have enough money," she agreed.

"I wish it was that easy," he said taking a deep breath.

"And why is it not?" Farren asked, yawning.

"Protocol, baby protocol," he told her drifting off to sleep.

"Did Christian know they were going to kill Carren, can you at least tell me that?" she asked.

"Well honestly, we thought they were coming for you."

"Me?"

"Yeah, you know the shit with your mom and all of that; no one wanted you to ever be able to sit at the Cartel."

"And Chrissy knew this?" Farren asked.

"Yeah, but he paid it no mind," James told her.

"So what do I have to do with Chrissy's bullshit and why did they have to kill my child?"

James shrugged his shoulders.

"I'll just ask my mom," Farren said.

He chuckled, "Good luck, because that lady has more secrets than anybody I know."

Farren didn't like that statement, especially since in her quiet time she was able to put so much shit together, which is when she realized that everyone had been trying to tell her all along about her mother. Dice. Jonte. Everyone except Christian.

"Why did Christian hate my mama so much, did he know who she was when he met me?" he asked.

"Not at first, but of course after a while he put two and two together."

"And he still stayed with me?" she asked surprised.

"He loved you, what you mean?" he asked.

"Hmmm," Farren was more confused than ever.

"So back to Carren," she changed the subject.

"Drop it," he told her.

"No, about my child? I shol in the hell wont," she told him.

"What you need to be doing is deciding how you about to handle this war," James said pointing at the dead bodies on the floor of Farren's garage.

"I'm not stunting them," she said.

"What you mean you not stunting them? You are not untouchable. Stop thinking that you are cus newsflash, these motherfuckers ran up in your house and you're supposed to be dead," he yelled.

"You don't think I know that!" she yelled back.

"No disrespect but you need to place your focus on the children that you have left and try your hardest to keep them alive," he said seriously.

Wow. That was a very hard pill for Farren to swallow. No words came out of her mouth because she didn't know what to say or think, but what she did know, is that James was speaking real shit.

"So what's the solution?" she asked.

Chanel peeped her head into the entryway of the garage.

"Babe, everything okay?" she asked.

James looked back at Farren.

Farren shook her head, "Oh hell no."

"Don't sleep on my babe," he said.

"What y'all talking about?" she asked.

Farren pulled out her gun and shot In her direction, barely missing her sister's head.

"BITCH," Chanel became enraged.

Farren smiled.

"Oh yeah, she the one."

Chanel passed Farren's test with flying colors. If she ducked and cried then she was weak, but she didn't. She was ready to pop off and that's what Farren was looking for.

"The one for what cus hoe, I'm about to whoop off in your ass," Chanel snapped.

Farren giggled. This was going to be so much fun. Less than two years ago, she was being dragged to the wilderness to prepare for The Roundtable. But unlike Farren, Chanel didn't have nearly as much time as Farren did. It was now or never, and they had to be in it to win it.

Chapter 8

Chanel woke up sweating; she could have sworn she heard her grandmother's voice whispering in her ear, telling her to RUN. Chanel had been having the same nightmare for a few weeks, she was unsure of the hidden message. Her "training" had been going well so far, it was more mental than physical and Chanel had to remind herself of that daily. Chanel laid back down wiping the sweat beads from her forehead. She was tired as fuck. Between balancing her business, training with Farren and James, and attempting to be the best mother and girlfriend she could be, she was extremely exhausted. There was never enough time in a day and she was constantly going from one place to the next. James stared at her and Chanel jumped.

"Shit you scared me! Why are you up?" she asked.

"Couldn't sleep, let's go for a walk," he told her, getting out of bed.

"A walk? I can barely use my legs to walk," she complained.

"Excuses are tools-"James started but Chanel finished, "are tools of incompetence that build monuments of nothing and those that excel in them, excel in nothing," she said.

"Good, now let's try this thing again," James smiled and got back in the bed, holding Chanel tight in his arms.

"Why am I doing this?" she asked after a few silent minutes had passed.

"If you have to ask then you shouldn't be doing it sweetie."

"I like it though. Ugh, I was just asking you a question off the record."

"I'm listening," he told her.

"Why did you join?" she asked.

Chanel and James had grown very close in the past few weeks, especially dealing with the death of her grandmother, but in the back of Chanel's head she still thought of Q, and she hated that she did because she was pretty sure he wasn't thinking of her at all. Chanel wanted to ask James what did he like about her and what made him want to spend his nights and mornings with her. Her insecurities were starting to settle in and she realized that they were on two totally different paths, but trying their hardest to coincide with one another.

James adored Chanel and he was completely oblivious to the fact that her feelings were very sketchy. He had confided in his family that she was the one and he planned on marrying her really soon. James wanted at least one son or daughter; well as long as the baby was healthy, he was happy. Chanel was IT for him, he felt honored that she saw fit to open up to him and he would do whatever he had to do to forever protect the love he "assumed" they shared for another.

"Nakia used to always make sure I was straight and one day I asked her can I protect her and she said yeah, been down ever since."

"So you don't know how to cook dope and all that?" Chanel asked.

"Nah."

"Do you regret getting involved with them?"

James shook his head. "No, my family has no wants, I don't have any either."

"But you could have easily gotten a job like regular people."

"Jobs weren't for people like me."

"And what does that mean? Am I different because I have a job?"

"You own your own business, what are you talking about? Why is everything an argument with you?" he asked, pushing himself away from Chanel.

"That's not what I was trying to do, just asking a question."

"You won't go far if you don't learn to start thinking before speaking," he told her, rolled over, and closed his eyes.

Chanel was growing tired of hearing the same thing from him and his sister. She was close to screaming from the top of her lungs, "I didn't ask to do this shit" but she never said anything. She would just bite her tongue and keep it moving.

The journey had not been easy at all. If Farren was rude and inconsiderate before, it was ten times worse now.

Chanel asked herself is this really what she wanted or was this what Farren wanted. Chanel was a grown ass woman and wanted to always keep herself and her child's best interest at heart. Chanel needed to get away and do some thinking. It wasn't that James had pressured her or begged her to do anything; she made this decision simply on her own but to be clear, money was her motive.

People did things for various reasons, power, respect, loyalty; well, Chanel Cavett cared about money. The almighty dollar bill is what kept her up at night, learning everything she needed to know to possibly be voted into the Cartel.

On the other side of town, Farren and Kool had just finished having some of the best fucking mind-blowing, screaming, in the gut, pussy creaming, toes curling, tracks slipping, eyes rolling, sex in the world.

Farren was still panting, her body was extremely sweaty, but she wanted more. She didn't want to stop getting fucked by him. Farren planted small kisses all over his body.

"Ain't no way you want some more," he said in disbelief.

"My pussy still jumping, feel it," she told him, taking his hand and placing it between her legs.

"Is it me or is it you?" he asked.

"It's me, I be missing you. I wish you would just move back here."

"We already had this talk," Kool told her getting out of bed and going into Farren's bathroom. She was right on his heels.

"Okay, and how many times do I have to tell you that shit will never happen again?"

"I'm good shawty, and we had a cool lil' night, don't ruin it," he warned.

"You don't tell me what the fuck to do, you need to move back here," she yelled. Kool yoked her up and Farren couldn't believe he had his hands wrapped around her neck. It took her back to when Christian Knight first found about her talking to Jonte.

"Stop talking to me like I'm your slave or some shit. If I said I wasn't moving back then that's what it is," he told her.

"Kool, get out of my house," she mumbled through the few breaths she was able to get in.

"Say no more," he said, still stepping in the shower.

"Now," she told him.

"Hey, if I'm going to leave here and go to the next bitch's house, I at least gotta make sure I don't smell like your pussy," he said.

Farren was pissed; she threw a vase at the wall.

"Man what is wrong with you?" he asked behind the glass shower door.

"You are what's wrong with me. You keep playing fucking mind games with me," she told him. Kool was listening to her, but not really, because even though she was getting older and had four children plus a few messed up surgeries, she was still flawless in his eyes. It was as if Farren could do no wrong. His dick got hard just thinking about how she was hurting behind his actions.

She wasn't a dummy and she definitely was telling the truth. Kool had been bullshitting around with Farren, but it was because Farren was one of those women that could easily make you fall on your knees and slide the ring on her finger. She had that poisonous effect about her and Kool had fell under her spell once, and he wasn't sure that if it happened again he would be able to make it out alive, or better yet, the same person he was before he even met her.

Kool got his shit together. After Farren supposedly killed him, it was hard for him to even fuck a bitch. No one compared to Farren.

Kool got out the shower and went towards her, but she walked out of the bathroom.

"Get out of my house, I mean that shit fuck nigga," she snapped.

"Aye shawty, watch your mouth, you know I don't like all of that," he told her.

"Fuck you," she told him straight up. Kool ignored her because he already knew what she wanted and what would get her acting right. Kool went into her closet and looked for something in particular.

"What are you doing?" she asked.

"Hush," he yelled from her closet.

He smiled and rubbed his hands together when he found them; he came back into her bedroom and pushed Farren down in the bed.

"Ummmm, what are you doing with my shoes, those are exclusive," she told him.

"You had these on when I first met you. I'm about to fuck you real good in these," he told her winking. Farren blushed. How did he remember what kind of shoes she had on, he acted like he wasn't even stunting her, but apparently he was.

Farren opened her legs and started pleasing herself, never taking her eyes off him.

"Hell yeah, talk that shit you was talking," he told her, sliding his dick in and out of her mouth.

Kool loved Farren's head; shawty was the certified truth. He never had to tell her what to do or how to do it; she always did it just right. Kool's eyes closed and he threw his head back and enjoyed the wet and warm sensation, baby girl was getting it. Farren never stopped sucking him off until she drained him of all of his nut.

"Lay back," he told her, taking his time, kissing every single inch of her body.

Farren taught Kool how to take his time with her. When they first started fucking, he just wanted to keep his clothes on and pull his dick out of the insert of his jeans and boxers, and Farren had to tell him, "oh no sir, I am not a skeezer, you gone get naked and eat this pussy from the back."

Farren was only as nasty as the man she was laying beside. If the nigga didn't put in work to please her, then she didn't either. Farren took pride in knowing that a lot of Kool's first was with her; she was getting him right and turning him into the perfect sex slave.

"Fuck yeah," she encouraged him to keep eating her pussy just how he was, cus he was tearing her shit up.

"Damn bae you taste good," he said in between slurps and licks.

"I know," Farren said cockily.

Knock.

Tap.

Tap.

Tap.

Tap.

Farren opened her eyes and Kool's dick went limp. Those were gunshots.

She got up so fast and threw on the closest thing to her, Kool searched for his jeans.

"You got a strap in here?" he asked.

She stopped and smirked at him. "Come on now boo, they'll never catch me slipping," she told him, throwing him a gun she had in the drawer of the nightstand. Farren pulled one from under the mattress.

"Go check on your kids," he told her.

Farren nodded. They unlocked the bedroom door and crept up out of the house. The alarm didn't go off so she wondered was it a drive by.

Farren kids were sleeping peacefully. Farren went downstairs and saw Kool with the door opened, tattoos covering every single inch of his body. His six-pack had dried up specs of Farren's cum on it. His True Religion jeans were barely on his waist. Farren hated a nigga that sagged, but that's just how he rolled. He didn't try to change her so she left him alone for the most part.

"Did you see anything?" she asked.

He closed the door, handed her a Ziploc bag and said, "You need to move."

Farren looked down and dropped the bag on the hardwood floor.

It was her teeth. Her fucking teeth.

MARIO.

That fucking pussy ass bitch brought blood to her steps, all over some pussy? He was hating that bad? Damn, Farren wasn't worried about him, but she was now questioning his character.

Kool was in the kitchen heating his food up from their dinner date earlier.

"What happened to you over there?" he asked.

"Nothing, I recovered there," she said.

"So them not your teeth in your mouth?" he asked.

Farren shook her head, she was just a tad bit embarrassed but it wasn't anything she could do. She was grateful that she still had her life, fuck them teeth.

Farren felt like that was a weak ass move on Mario's part. He was basically throwing everything he ever did for her in her face.

Farren remembered being so hurt when she finally looked at herself after waking up from the coma.

"Farren, the doctors promised that all of it can be fixed," Mario rubbed her back.

Her mouth was wide open but no sound came out, she couldn't react. Her face was bruised, swollen, and she didn't even look the same, it was as if someone had purposely whooped her ass for no reason.

"I am ugly," she finally cried out.

"Farren," he tried to comfort her.

"Shut the fuck up," Farren told him. She pushed him out of the bathroom and closed and locked the door. The hospital staff pitied Mario. She had been a complete bitch these past few days, and everyone liked her more when she was in a coma.

Once Farren awakened, she requested fresh linen sheets and not just another pair of sheets from the closet. She made Mario go find her top-of-the line sheets along with ostrich-feather stuffed pillows, Farren wasn't playing no games.

Farren touched her face and cringed at the pain that was running through her jaws. The bags that had formed under her eyes were extremely dark. Her grill was fucked up and the few teeth she did have left, needed to be pulled. Greg had knocked her in the face with his gun and you could tell. She had bruises all around her mouth and on her neck.

Although Farren was thankful for life, she still couldn't believe she was stuck in this predicament. Ever since Farren was a little girl she had been told how beautiful she was, but looking in the mirror, she damn sure didn't see any of those breathtaking features.

Farren felt bad for complaining about her image when she should have been thanking God she was alive. Farren's legs were weak and she had to use a cane to get out of bed. Her legs still felt like noodles but she was trying her hardest to regain her independence, although she had a very long way to go before she would be Farren Knight again.

Farren wanted to scream, pout, shout, and cry but what would that do? It wouldn't repair her mouth, face, or the broken ribs. It wouldn't do anything. Farren was all out of emotion and she really had no more fucks to give.

"So you were dead and they brought you back alive?" he asked.

She shook her head. "From what I had been told, my heartbeat was just really faint and I was losing a lot of blood really fast," she said.

Kool shook his head. "Damn baby," he pulled her into him. Farren was tight, she wasn't comfortable and Kool saw it all on her face.

"What's wrong?" he asked.

She pulled away from him and went to pull out her coffee pot. Since they were up and alert, might as well make a big ass breakfast.

"I don't feel like myself anymore, my sister...she don't know what the fuck she doing at all," she admitted.

"So why are you even putting her in that predicament?" he was very confused.

"Because...this might sound selfish, but I don't give a fuck. I need her to get her money up so my kids can be straight."

"Okay, put some money in her account for them, but Farren, everybody is damn near dead, what's going to happen to you?" he asked.

Farren wanted to change the subject; she didn't feel like having this very serious talk.

"You don't get what I'm saying, just go lay down or something I'm about to cook I'm hungry."

"Man I get what you saying but you ain't gotta go about it like this."

"I'm getting her right."

"She's not you, don't forget that," he told her, kissing her cheek and walking off.

Farren took a deep breath. She knew her boo was telling the truth and Farren needed to talk to James without Chanel around. Farren was a woman that always trusted her gut, since it never failed her. She was worried that her days were numbered, especially with the death of Kim and soon to be Mario's ass. Farren wasn't appreciative of him leaving teeth and shit, or shooting her house up. If you want to kill her, come at her.

Farren called his phone and surprisingly the crazy motherfucker answered the phone.

"Farren Knight, wassup?" he said surprisingly.

"Hi, how are you?" she played this mind game with him.

"I'm well and you?"

"Blessed, living good, you know how I do," Farren said cockily.

Mario laughed, "I'm assuming you got my little treat," he came on out and said.

"Really Mario?" she questioned.

"Hey, no disrespect, but you don't want to fuck with me."

"And what did I do to you?" she asked.

"You used me and for that you will pay. I am not a toy," he told her and hung up the phone.

Farren shook her head, she wasn't scared at all. See, Mario messed up on numerous categories. Farren was a listener, she listened before she spoke. Farren would watch her friends in college sit up and tell all their business, and Farren would barely mumble a word or two.

She never really had anything to say because she had always been private, and on the real, Farren had always been a little sneaky something, so she didn't need bitches in her business fucking up her flow with Dice.

Farren smiled evilly at the things she could do to destroy Mario's little life, his downfall was that he was a pillow talker. Farren hated a nigga that pillow talked. Any man that she ever really gave her heart to was private. Farren believed that as a man, if a problem did surface, any and everything should be done to make sure the situation is taken care of. Mario whined, worried, and complained to Farren, she knew more about his empire than she should have for two important reasons. One, she was technically considered competition and two, her last name was not Sanchez.

It was nothing for Farren to make one phone call to some young hungry niggas in Hardy Projects who desperately needed a come-up. All she had to do was provide them with the time and location and let them handle the rest.

Farren could ruin Mario's whole operation in a matter of one hour, he better tread lightly.

Farren opened her notebook and jotted down a to-do list. Once she wrote down fresh roses for Carren, Jonte, Dice and Chrissy, she sat the pen down and took another sip of coffee. She couldn't believe she had lost so many people. Farren told herself every single day if it wasn't for her children, she would have been slit her wrist. Life had no meaning to her, she was seriously praying for better days.

Farren didn't have much time to shower and get to training with Chanel. She was super late and she hated being late. Farren made sure no one was following her before she turned into the gun range. James had a good friend out in Forest Park, Georgia who owned a gun range and had been letting them use it every morning for one hour.

Farren heard James yelling at Chanel when she knocked on the back door requesting entrance. Chanel ran to the door, she rolled her eyes. "He's getting on my nerves already and we only been here for seven minutes."

Farren laughed. "Good morning to you too, sis."

Farren took her scarf from around her neck and removed her shades.

"What's the problem?" she asked. James looked extremely frustrated, his long arm extended towards the glass window.

Farren went closer to get a better view; Chanel's ass missed every single point.

"Chanel, are you shooting with your eyes closed?" Farren asked.

"You know what little Miss James Bond, let me see you shoot," she said agitated. They were always getting on her, it never failed. In their eyes she couldn't do shit right.

Farren smirked. She pulled out her own gun from the back of her pants. Chanel tried to hand her the headphones and shades.

"No need baby, let me show you how a real bitch does this," she winked.

James shook his head in awe. Farren's ass was so cocky it was ridiculous.

She imagined the paper man being MARIO since he was the newest target on her menu, and Farren lit that damn paper up. She had gotten so used to using her gun that the force of the shot didn't knock her out of her stance. She put the gun down like it was nothing and pulled out her iPhone to email the lady back about Morgan starting piano lessons on Thursdays around five.

Chanel was shocked. "How did you do that? Please teach me. We been coming here for weeks and I still can't shoot at all," she complained.

Farren took a deep breath trying to see how she can tell her sister the truth without starting an argument, because Chanel was always in defensive mode.

"Stop thinking so much, don't worry about trying to please James," she said.

James spoke up, "It's not me she trying to please."

Farren turned around and looked at James. "What you trying to say?"

"You already know what I'm saying."

Farren spoke to Chanel, "Is it hard for you to focus when I'm around?"

Chanel hated when they made her feel like she was a child.

"No need to be embarrassed boo, business is business, we trying to get you right," Farren told her.

Chanel nodded her head.

Farren smiled. "Y'all call me if y'all need me," she said and left the gun range.

James stood and rubbed Chanel's back.

"Come on... open your legs, pull your shoulders back, and take a deep breath, but listen to me carefully. Sometimes you won't have time to take a deep breath and all that; you just gotta shoot to save your life." James stood behind her and coached her to perform a perfect shot.

Chanel took a deep breath and shot.

Her eyes closed instantly when the bullet left the chamber, but when she opened them it was a shot to the head.

"Good job, but with your eyes closed how you don't know if it's a bullet coming your way?" he asked.

"Do it again," he told her.

Chanel looked back at him and kissed his cheek. "Stop man focus," James told her.

Chanel rolled her eyes and shot again, this time she missed.

"This is still good, you at least got him to drop his gun cus you caught him in his shoulder," he told her.

"Okay, let me try again," she told him.

About thirty minutes later, Chanel had made more progress in that time than she had in the past few weeks. James was so proud of her.

"You might just get some head when we get home," he teased.

Chanel rolled her eyes. "I wish."

James had her on a strict no sex, no meat, no phones or social media, and no television regime. Chanel's ass couldn't do shit but go to work and come home and train.

"Oh shit, I have to go. I'm going to be late for work," Chanel told James, handing him the gun and running into the bathroom to switch out of her all black and into her business professional attire.

Chanel didn't care how much training they asked her to do, she never ever let it come before her job. Chanel's profession meant everything to her and she made sure that both James and Farren knew she didn't play about The Cavett Agency.

Chapter 9

"How you got that fine ass man staying with you and you don't even know how to boil a pot of water for eggs? Move over," Nakia fussed at Chanel.

Chanel had been trying her hardest but Nakia didn't budge. She didn't like her at all and didn't hide her feelings.

Chanel ignored her complaints about her lack of expertise around the kitchen; she went to sit in the living room. She didn't understand why they couldn't just have the barbeque at Farren's house, but she insisted on wanting to be around love on July 4.

Chanel lifted her shirt up to wipe the sweat off her forehead. It was hot as hell in Nakia's tiny apartment, but it was even hotter outside in the courtyard. Chanel continued to peep out of the window to make sure her daughter, Madison was safe and sound.

"Get out of my blinds, nobody messing with your lil' pot belly child," Nakia told her, licking the wooden spoon she used to stir the baked beans.

"Watch it," Chanel warned.

"Or what?" Nakia shot back.

Chanel walked out of the apartment and went to the courtyard. She'd rather be hot and musty than sit up under Nakia.

"Chanel, you shoulda brought some water out here, it's hot as hell," Neeki said.

"Where is Farren?" she asked.

"Out there playing with the kids," Neeki told her, refocusing on her card game with all the locals in the courtyard.

"Whew it's hot," Chanel said sitting down.

Farren came over. "Y'all wanna jump rope?" she asked.

"Girl hell nah, I'm too old," Chanel said laughing.

"I'm way older than you...come on!" she pulled Chanel out to the middle of the courtyard.

"Go mama," Madison cheered Chanel on while Morgan and Noel cheered their mama on.

"Come on let's go, keep it up, keep it up," Farren encouraged Chanel.

"Girl, ooh, my legs cramping up," Chanel said.

"Come on sis," Farren laughed and giggled.

She was having the time of her life. Farren didn't care how much money she made or how many countries she visited, Hardy Projects always had her heart on lock. She loved the hood she grew up in and didn't hide it.

Farren remembered when the college she attended to receive her Bachelor's degree, invited her back as one of the top ten alumni. Her speech was in honor of every black woman that ever went through something and came out on top.

First, let me say it is an honor to stand before so many of my colleagues, my professors, friends, and line sisters, but I wouldn't be standing here if it wasn't for the grace of God. I am nothing without Him. I am Farren Knight, a proud graduate of Lincoln University; I am also a product of my environment. I was raised in poverty, section-8, rat and roach infested apartments, all of that. But today, I am a very successful commercial attorney; I'm the proud wife to my husband and best friend, Christian Knight and the mother of three children. In my spare time, I like to come to events like these and share my personal testimony, in hopes that I can encourage one of you out there to be all that you can be. Whether you're here on a scholarship, student loans, or if your parents are paying for you to get an education, never lose sight of your goals. I was one of those children where all the odds were against me. My mother was a single mother, who had a chip on her shoulder, and I grew up never seeing her smile or hearing the words 'I love you'. At the time, my father would send checks to help my mom out and she would never use the money. I suffered for years off something I had nothing to do with. But let me tell you something, I never gave up. Even when my classes got hard and I failed a few finals, I never gave up. As much as I loved my hood, I knew I couldn't return there. My sister and I both said we would never live there again, and we didn't. After graduating high school, we both never looked back.

I can go to Hardy now and have a good ole time, donate old clothes, and furniture because God has put me in a position to be a blessing. I would like to encourage you beautiful ladies today, to stay focused and get that degree. Knowledge is the one thing man cannot take from you.

A gunshot going off snapped Farren out of her thoughts. Noel screamed, "Ma." Farren's heart was beating and she was trying to process the gunshot and the direction in which she heard it; it was her mother's building.

Chanel ran to get the kids. No one in Hardy panicked because gunshots were normal.

Neeki yelled to Farren, "Where the fuck is mama?"

"The...house...the house," Farren mumbled.

She prayed that the gunshot came from the neighborhood behind them and not Hardy Projects. Farren and her sister took the steps to get to her mom's apartment. No one was in there, Farren was relieved.

Chanel and the kids came up the steps out of breath, Farren asked, "Why would you bring them up here?" she snapped.

"I'm not from here, where were we supposed to go?" Chanel yelled.

Neeki said, "Farren, stop yelling at her she ain't know."

"Where is mama?" Farren went into the apartment and came out not seeing her mother.

"Was she outside?" Farren asked.

Neeki shook her head.

Farren noticed the bloody handprints on the wall, and she thought for a second.

Farren pulled her gun out and her children gasped. Michael had seen his mama hold a gun a few times, he wasn't surprised. In his eyes, his mama was cool as hell for even carrying one.

The other house, Farren thought to herself.

Farren took a few steps two doors down and across the hall.

"Farren, don't go in there," Chanel said.

"You think I'm about to leave my mama in there, really?" Farren said, shocked. She shook her head. Ain't no way Chanel was ready to sit at The Roundtable; she had too much pussy in her heart.

"Come on Neeki," Farren told her.

Neeki opened the door and ran to her mama who was sprawled out on the floor, blood pouring from her stomach.

Farren checked the apartment. "Ma is anybody in here?" she asked.

"No," she whispered with tears in her eyes.

Farren yelled out the door, "Chanel call the ambulance," she said.

"Don't waste no money on no ambulance," Nakia said, coughing up blood.

Farren looked out the window, looking for any vehicles speeding out of the complex.

"Ma, who did this?" Neeki cried.

"Farren, come here," she said.

Farren went to her mother, her mind was on revenge. She figured her mother was dying so there was nothing she really could do about that. It sounded horrible, but Farren had grown immune to people leaving here, it didn't even bother her no more.

"What happened?"

"Listen," she said. Nakia knew she didn't have a lot of time left.

"Christian was not who you think he was...but Mario is," Nakia said, eyes slowly rolling to the back of her head.

"Huh? What? Ma!" Farren started shaking her mother's body.

Neeki yelled at her, "Farren she's gone."

"Shut up!" she shouted.

"Maaaaaaaa," she cried.

What in the fuck was she referring to, what did that mean? Farren had no idea and she needed answers.

"Mama please," Farren begged, but it was too late.

Three hours later, Chanel came into the room. "Hey sis, I'm going to take the kids to my house, you okay?" she asked.

Farren nodded.

She had taken a bath and changed into some comfortable clothes. It was a little difficult washing her mother's blood off her hands, but it wouldn't be the first time she did that either.

Her hair was piled on top of her head in a bun, and her Fendi frames graced her face. Farren had a lot of thinking to do and after she had spoken to the police and handled everything with her mother's body, it was time to get to work.

"Okay, well I will be here in the morning," Chanel said.

"That's Spider, my baby daddy's best friend, he's going to make sure y'all get home safe," Farren told Chanel and walked off. She didn't have much conversation right now.

Neeki was cleaning the blood up off the floor. Hardy was a mess; everybody was mourning and crying. Nakia would truly be missed. She was raised here by her mother and had raised her children here as well. She may not have been the nicest, but she was loved and appreciated, and always did as much as she could for others. Nakia loved cooking on Sundays and anybody was welcome to a plate. She played poker on Mondays and Wednesdays, and shot dice on Friday nights. Hardy Projects was the highlight of Nakia's life; she would wake up and sit in her windowsill for hours before starting her day.

"What made mama run in here?" Neeki asked.

Farren turned around, "What you say?"

"I'm saying, I wonder what made her run in this apartment, it's empty," Neeki said, mopping the floor.

Farren stood and thought.

"Think Farren, think," she tapped her forehead.

Farren went through the apartment, but it wasn't that big and there wasn't anything there or was it? Farren took her time, opening cabinets, closets, drawers, nothing.

Farren never really understood why her mother kept this apartment anyway. After Neeki was done cleaning, they locked the door with the key that was found on the floor by the elevator. Something was off but Farren knew that she would figure it out sooner or later.

Farren and her sister sat in the living room, not really wanting to be around a bunch of emotional people right now. Neeki wasn't crying and Farren wasn't either, but one would have to really understand how they were raised to catch their drift.

"Mama was mean as hell," Neeki blurted out after a few hours of them sitting in silence, wrapped up in their thoughts.

"Girl who is you telling? She was way more mean to me than she was to you," Farren said.

"That's cus your ass was fast," Neeki said laughing.

"Nah, she was just hating cus ain't nobody want her."

"I can't believe this shit."

"And on July 4th at that," Farren agreed with her sister.

Her mother loved holidays in the courtyard. That's when everybody pulled up and shared laughs and old memories.

"Who do you think did it?" Neeki asked.

Farren took a deep breath, "I'm not sure yet," she lied.

Farren knew exactly who the fuck did this shit and his days were extremely numbered.

Her mother wasn't the best, that's for sure, but at the end of the day, she was still their mama.

Farren cuddled up with her sister and they spent the night watching all of their mom's favorite movies and drinking Hennessy, her favorite alcoholic beverage.

"How are you?" Chanel whispered into her sister's ear four days later at the gravesite. Many of the members of The Cartel was present and even Diane, Farren's stepmother, came to show her respects.

"I'm good, why you ask?" Farren whispered back.

"Uh, we're at your mother's funeral and you haven't shed not one tear," she said.

"Tears are for weak people, she knew that I loved her," Farren said and walked off.

Chanel shook her head; Farren was a fucking nut case. She watched her sister grace the grounds of the funeral, hugging people and kissing cheeks. She moved with not much effort. Everything she did seemed perfect, as if she never made any mistakes.

Chanel often wondered when she would get it together. She had been doing her training but still felt like she wasn't making enough progress in time for the meeting, which was in a few weeks, less than three to be exact.

They rode in the car together with the children in the back seat. "Are you okay?" Chanel asked again, for the millionth time that week.

Farren took a deep breath, "After I lost my best friend, I stopped crying when people leave me."

"I hate that you keep going through so much shit. I wouldn't wish all of this pain on my worst enemy," Chanel told her sincerely.

Farren smiled and took her sister's hand in hers, and they made their way to the Hamptons. Farren just wanted to get away with her family and spend some much needed quality time with her boo and her children. She knew that a war would be starting soon. Kim's family was looking for her body, but the good thing was that no one knew how much Kim hated Farren so she was the last suspect on the list, and she prayed to God that it stayed that way. Farren didn't need any more problems coming her way. After The Roundtable, she just wanted to move to London and raise her children; she was so over living in the United States, it had nothing to offer her but bullshit on top of bullshit.

Behind Farren's Range Rover was James and Kool sharing a blunt. "Man, I can't believe Farren's mama is dead. I been knowing that crazy ass lady for years," Kool said.

James nodded his head in agreement. He wasn't an emotional ass nigga but when Chanel called with the news, he definitely shed a few tears. It hurt him to hear that the lady who had did so much for him had died. James remembered when she asked him to go work under Christian Knight.

"Who do they have you with now?" she asked, after handing James a cup of coffee.

She appreciated that James stopped by and showed her love every now and then, but she had taught him to be loyal so she wasn't surprised by his warm gestures.

"I been working at the house," he told her.

Everything on her face looked surprised. "At the house? Doing what? You not a cook or a maid," Nakia scoffed.

"Bianchi just making sure everything taken care of with the cameras and screening people because the Roundtable is coming up," he explained.

"Hmm... well there is a fella coming through, he's a little older than you. I need you to let me know if he's chosen," she told James.

"What's his name? Cus I think they have already filled Dice's seat."

"I bet they didn't waste any time. I don't care what nobody says, Bianchi had that boy killed," Nakia shook her head. Dice's death hurt her more than anything; she really loved him and considered him a son.

"It's been some speculation about that, but of course he says his kid was at home when it happened," James told Nakia.

"Fucking liars," she spat.

"What's the dude's name?" James asked, staying on task. Whenever he came to visit Nakia, the only thing she wanted to discuss was how raggedy the Cartel was and how they weren't seeing any real money.

"Christian...Knight. Christian Knight, real gentlemen, which is what the Cartel needs, some fucking class," she said, lighting a cigarette.

"Christian Knight, I'll be on the lookout," he told her.

Nakia always knew everything before it happened, it never failed. James would definitely miss her unedited truth. She never had a problem speaking on how she felt and didn't care whether your feelings were hurt or not.

"What made you leave?" Kool asked James.

"After Christian went to jail, I was done. I only stayed cus of him, the rest of them niggas lame," James told Kool.

"I keep telling Farren, leave that shit alone, but she won't listen," Kool said.

"Are you in a position to take care of her?" he asked. Kool was cool and all but James knew the nigga's money wasn't long, and he wouldn't be surprised if Farren was taking care of his ass.

"Nah, but I know how to get my money up, I'm just laying low right now," Kool said.

James nodded his head and smirked. He wasn't trying to mess with the man's ego, so he decided to just turn the radio up.

A weekend in the Hamptons was just what the doctor ordered for the family. Chanel and Farren were out back on the balcony, sipping wine and watching the sun set, while the children watched a scary movie. It was Kool and James' night to cook dinner but they were too occupied with a game of pool in the basement.

"How did you know you were in love?" Chanel asked.

"Girl, you and all these questions," Farren joked.

Chanel threw her napkin at her big sister, "Bitch shut up and answer the question."

Farren laughed, "Ooh, don't make me laugh too hard, you know my stomach fucked up," Farren said, half-joking, half telling the truth. Her body was not doing well at all and she seriously needed to visit the doctor soon.

"Hmm...love...okay, let's go back sis. What is love to you and do you love yourself?" she asked.

Chanel exhaled, "Whew I need a blunt, why you always asking me interview questions?"

"Girl I know you not talking!" Farren laughed.

"I don't know what love is, but I do love myself, but I love myself even more now than I ever have. I didn't think my life would be this way, designer shit that a nigga didn't buy for me, I copped it myself, going to beautiful places with my fly ass big sister-"

"That's not loving yourself though. All of this can be taken away in a matter of a few seconds, so then what?" Farren asked.

Chanel paused and thought about what her sister had said. "Well I do love myself, I do know that."

"Okay, what do you love about yourself?" Farren asked.

"I'm still here. Man, I am still here. I was addicted to coke and it could have taken me from my daughter a few times, but I'm still here," she said with tears in her eyes.

"Wow," Farren said, laying her head back on the lawn chair.

"Yeah I know," Chanel said with dignity. God made a way out of no way for her and she was forever thankful, plus she had a praying grandmother who wasn't letting the devil take her baby. Chanel wasn't too proud of the things she had done in her past, but she was a changed woman now. The only thing she secretly needed to work on now was her confidence and the ability to think for herself.

Chanel always needed validation, and she didn't want to feel that way.

"I love myself because I'm sexy as hell and I know it," Farren said.

Chanel looked at her sister. "Are you high?"

Farren laughed, "Yeah, but so what, I'm still telling the truth," she winked.

"Girl you are crazy."

"I want to experience real love, like some 'no matter what' shit," she said.

"Love is intense, sis."

"I don't care, I want that extreme love."

"I think I'm done with love," Farren admitted.

"I can tell," Chanel said.

"You can? How?"

"You just seem like nothing matters to you anymore."

"It don't."

"So what are you and Kool doing besides wasting each other's time?" Chanel asked.

"Having some of the best fucking sex ever," Farren said happily.

"Ewww."

"Girl, ain't no eww over here honey cus I'm the truth in bed, and I love young niggas," Farren said truthfully.

"He's like fifteen years younger than you, that's gross."

"Okay bitch, don't point the finger cus James ass is knocking on fifty if he ain't already," Farren said.

"It's different with him."

"Ain't nothing different, pussy is pussy, dick is dick."

"What if Kool tells you he loves you, what you gone do?"

"He won't, trust me, I tried to kill him, that nigga can never love me," Farren said. She had accepted that they wouldn't be much of anything no matter how much she apologized.

"You don't know that," Chanel told her.

"I do and it's okay because guess what? I don't even care! I have experienced so much love in my lifetime that if I never meet another I will be okay," Farren stated.

"Wow."

"I'm serious though. Like, I have experienced love in three different ways, with three totally different men, and it was all beautiful, not perfect, but very, very memorable."

"I love James but I still love Q too, is that bad? Does that make me an idiot?"

"Not at all, the heart wants what it wants, make no apologies for that," Farren told her.

"Ugh, I don't know what to do, I want to find him and just talk to him," she said.

"Be careful what you ask for," Farren told her.

She stood up. "I'm hungry let me go check on the food cus I don't smell nothing cooking," Farren said and went back in the house.

Chapter 10

"Jerome, do we have any makeup artists in the directory that does not require us to break the bank with this budget?" Chanel asked in frustration. She was tired and needed rest. Her legs were aching from the two miles her and Farren ran this morning, on top of being stuck in traffic for almost two hours and getting to the office late. Chanel was irritated and needed food, but with her next event being less than four days away, food was the last thing on her to-do list.

"I can ask my cousin Pooh," he said.

Chanel glanced up at him to see if he was joking, because now was not the time to be laughing; time was of the essence.

"Does she have any pictures we can look at?" Chanel questioned.

"Let me go to her Instagram," he pulled out his cell phone. Chanel rubbed the sides of her head, massaging her temple. She felt a headache rising and all she wanted to do was take a bubble bath and cuddle up with her daughter and James and watch something funny on television. Chanel was stressing, she saw Farren calling her and sent the call to ignore; she didn't have any free time to talk. Farren's ass was already rich and she didn't do shit all day but online shop and water plants in her garden. Chanel still had bills every month that came and she worried. Although her business was doing extremely well, there were so many hands sticking in her pot that after payroll was taken care of, she barely saw any profit.

Chanel wanted Farren to look at the monthly numbers, but she didn't want to hear her fuss about the contract that Chanel had signed with the investors. She knew that it was some bogus shit, but at the time, she was extremely desperate to be a business owner.

"Okay, yeah, call her up, we can do sixty-five a face and a one hundred dollar travel fee," Chanel told Jerome.

She laid her head down on her desk...she just needed a few minutes of shut-eye.

"I see you still running yourself crazy," a voice woke her up from the nap she was attempting to take.

Chanel knew that voice and she just knew that the voice wasn't coming from him...

"What are you doing here?" she asked, pulling her gun from her purse quickly.

Q noticed what she was doing, and closed her office door.

"Oh, your sister must have taught you that lil' trick?" Q snickered.

Chanel couldn't deny how good he looked. She figured he must have gotten his act together and got off the drugs...but why?

"How can I help you?" she asked.

"You owe me, no point in beating around the bush."

"Owe you what?" she asked, voice full of attitude.

"Everything, you had me raising that damn baby knowing she wasn't mine and a whole bunch of other shit, don't get me started," he said matter-of-factly.

"Quincy, you are funny as hell to me," she said, flipping through some mail that her assistant left on her desk.

"Do you still love me Coco?" he asked.

"No," she said quickly.

"I won't be broke no more and you gone make sure that I get what I need to come up," he slammed his hand on her desk.

"What you need to do is get your own damn money and get out of here," Farren's voice came from nowhere.

Chanel was happy that her sister did pop up at her office, because she didn't know what to do next. Q pumped so much fear in her heart it was ridiculous.

"Hmm hmm...Farren Knight. Yeah, I done heard about you...but you ain't as bad as Christian Knight said you was," he said licking his lips.

Farren Knight, one certified bad bitch stood before him, and even in pain, she still looked and felt like a billion dollars. Dressed in all white as usual, her hair was freshly washed and pressed by the Dominicans, eyebrows plucked and arched to perfection, teeth on fleek and body banging. Farren was in a league of her own and even on Quincy's best day, if he ever had one, he would never ever be able to capture the attention of Farren Knight and for that, he hated her.

Farren licked her lips and stepped into his personal space. "Wouldn't you like to know exactly what Christian Knight was talking about, cus I'm sure I was his favorite subject," she said.

Q took a deep breath and turned around. "I will be in touch, Coco."

Farren called out, "Her name is Chanel not Coco," she said and sat down in one of the chairs in Chanel's office.

"I've been calling you," she said.

"Busy, still busy so what's up?" Chanel said with an attitude.

"Is something wrong?" Farren asked.

"Why did you come in here acting like you own the place, this is my office not yours," she snapped.

Farren stood. "Oh boo boo, I know that tone all too well," she said, wagging her finger. Chanel noticed she was back wearing her engagement ring, the bitch was so confused.

"Farren I'm busy, what did you want?" she asked.

"Don't worry about it, let me let you get back to work," she told her.

Farren turned around at the entryway of the door. "Do not let this nigga knock you off your square, you have too much to lose," she said.

"Lose? Why? Because you need me? Besides that, what do you think I have to lose? Look around, I'm good," Chanel flaunted.

Farren shot her the 'bitch please' smile.

"Chanel, you and I both know that's not true," Farren said and left the office.

As she predicted, Quincy was lingering around the parking lot waiting on her or Chanel, she wasn't sure.

"I'm not my sister, I will kill you so get the fuck back," Farren told him in a very serious tone.

Q laughed, "I'm not worried," he said.

"You should be," Farren told him.

"Coco is mine. Before you came around she belonged to me and I'm back to get her."

"In case you forgot, she came looking for me. I didn't even know the bitch existed," Farren told him, unlocked her door and got in, never taking her hand off her razor. Farren had no problem gutting this nigga like a damn fish. She was quenching for blood and Q would do until she got her hands on Mario.

Farren hopped on the highway to meet Kool for lunch. She was twenty minutes late but he hadn't called or texted, which told her that he, too, was late. Farren whipped her Bentley Coupe into the nearest parking space. She made sure nothing was out of the ordinary before focusing her attention on her appearance. She added a fresh coat of red lipstick and dabbed some perfume behind her ear and wrist before stepping out, right as Kool was headed to the door of Legal Seafood.

"I knew you were late," she said.

"I had to handle something for my mama."

"I bet they can't wait 'til you move back here," she added, telling the hostess table for two.

"Give me a hug man," he told her. Farren smiled and gave him a hug. She brought her hands together around his neck and that's when she noticed she had the ring Jonte gave her on.

Oh shit, she thought to herself. When they pulled away, Farren struggled to get the ring off and tossed it into her purse.

Kool swore up and down Farren really wasn't stunting him and that ring would only confirm his allegations.

Farren felt the same way he did, but she didn't feel like arguing with him. She just wanted to eat good and kick back with her favorite guy at the moment.

"You smell good," he told her, holding one of her ass cheeks in his hands as they were escorted to the table.

"Let me sit right there," Farren told him.

"Nah, I can't have my back to the door," Kool told her.

"Okay me neither," she argued.

"I got you," he told her.

Farren shook her head, "Let me get that seat Kool."

"Farren, you don't trust me?" he asked.

"Nigga apparently you don't trust me either, you won't get up."

"I got you for real boo," he told her.

"No," she said. "Scoot over," she told him. Kool shook his head. "What I gotta do you for to trust me?" he asked.

"It's not you, it's me, I'm paranoid as hell," she told him.

"I do want to be with you," he told her.

"Kool shut the fuck up, you're so bipolar," Farren brushed him off.

"Damn for real, that's how it is?" he asked.

"One day you with me the next day you not. I'm not going back and forth with you, I'm just not," she told him.

"I'm going to show you baby," he told her, kissing her cheek and rubbing her thigh. Farren closed her eyes. His touch did something to her.

"You good shawty?" he asked.

"Yes, let's order." Farren snapped out of her thoughts of how good he ate her pussy and fucked her to sleep.

Kool laughed, "Order for me you know what daddy like," he said, texting on his cell phone. Farren stopped checking niggas' phones a long time ago. She didn't believe in going to look for dirt. In her eyes, a nigga will always be a nigga.

They were getting down on their oysters, fried catfish, and calamari, when one of the members of the Cartel slid into their booth across from them.

Farren had her gun in the middle of her and Kool so she was super straight.

"July 28, are you aware that your attendance has been requested but has not been confirmed?"

Farren nodded.

"See you soon," he said and got out of the booth before anything else could be exchanged.

"What the fuck was that?" Kool asked.

"Nothing."

"Why they coming after you?" Kool questioned.

"They not...it's no leader and they want me there, but I'm not fucking with that shit no more," she whispered.

"And you really think your sister is ready?" he asked. Kool wanted to tell her that Chanel wasn't built for that shit but that wasn't his business.

Farren looked in his eyes, appearing really hopeless. "I hope like hell she is or if not, I'm fucked," Farren said.

--

Three days later, dumb ass Chanel had been holed up in a two-star hotel fucking Q's brains out. She had an event tonight and had no plans on even going. In-between her legs were extremely sore and all she wanted was a bottle of cold water and a bath. Quincy hadn't given her a break yet, he was giving her that DICK nonstop. "Okay, just give me a second, please.....move," she told him, but he was still using his limp dick to hump her.

"Come on man," he moaned.

"You're not even hard, get off of me," she shouted and pushed him off. Quincy became enraged and backhanded her. Chanel fell off the bed, her head hitting the nightstand and she felt blood gush out of her nose.

"Never again." She heard herself say the same words she said the last time he had hit her.

"Why did you hit me?" she cried.

"Shut the fuck up," he told her.

Chanel didn't even bother going back and forth with him. Her head was hurting and her phone wouldn't stop ringing. It was her company calling and she knew she needed to get up and head that way, but her head was spinning.

Chanel tried to stand five minutes later and her head was still banging, but she couldn't let her employees down, she just couldn't. They had been planning this very important event for some time now.

"You better be coming right back too," Q threatened.

Chanel couldn't believe she had been ignoring James' calls for this sorry, evil ass nigga, but it was something about Quincy that she couldn't let go of. She needed to let him go, she just couldn't. It was as if Q had put roots on her pussy or something. Chanel had allowed the time, and most importantly the memories, she had made with James in the last few months disappear. Chanel didn't even realize that she was spiraling out of control. Although she wasn't participating with Quincy when he hit the blunt or snorted a few lines, didn't mean that she wouldn't start back eventually.

If her grandmother was alive, she would be so disappointed in Chanel. It was always Quincy that fucked Chanel up every single time. Chanel would do well but then somehow the wrath of Q would knock her off her track.

Across the street, Chanel and James were sitting in a rental watching Chanel, the dummy, which is the name they had given her a few days ago.

"She's a fucking idiot," Farren spat.

"You ain't lied," James said. He was so embarrassed. James had told his family about Chanel and had recently spoke with Farren about going to get an engagement ring, and here this dumb bitch was ducked off in the hood being a thot.

"She is in no position to be doing nothing with them, like, I don't play about my money," Farren snapped.

"I think she still is ready, it's just this nigga, gotta get rid of him," James said.

"You got more faith in her than I do," Farren mumbled.

Chanel stumbled in the house after her event. She couldn't go back to that hotel, she needed a bath and to brush her teeth. In the back of her head, she knew Q didn't give a fuck about her, what nigga who claimed to love and care about "his" woman, would fuck her seventy-two hours straight, pussy damn sure wasn't clean. Chanel had dried-up cum all in between her legs, she felt disgusting. She knew her employees were talking about her. She ran into her office one hour before the event started and took a hoe bath and threw on a wrinkled dress that she found in a Marshall's bag in her trunk.

Chanel owed all of them an apology and planned on stopping to get a handful of gift cards before returning to work. She locked her front door and slid her feet out of the pumps that had her toes trapped all night.

"Whew," she said, feeling relieved.

"How was the event?" James asked, sitting in the dark in a corner of her sitting room.

"Oh my God you scared me, what are you doing here?" she asked, holding her heart.

"Who did you think was making sure Madison got to summer camp since you been out whoring?" he came right out and asked.

Chanel was very shocked at his harsh tone, but not surprised that he was aware of where she had been. James was smart as fuck and a little psycho.

"James-" Chanel started.

"Save it, I'm not the one to play with and before I let that nigga destroy what we are building, I will kill him so your best bet is to nip it in the bud," he told her.

He prepared to leave but stopped once he got near her and whispered in her ear, "I want to hold you so bad and promise you everything he can't, but I don't believe in wasting my time," he told her, kissing her cheek and leaving her home.

Chanel's hands trembled and her keys and cell phone fell to the floor, she was so confused it was ridiculous. She didn't know what to do. How in the hell did she allow Quincy's dumb ass to come into her life and wreck everything she had worked so hard for? Her staff pointed fingers and whispered the entire night, Chanel was not much of a help at tonight's event and when she was asked to do the closing remarks, the lights only triggered her headache and she stumbled and mumbled the entire time she had the microphone in her hands.

Chanel sat in her bathtub for hours, until the water became ice cold. She didn't know what to do. It wasn't that she didn't love James, she just had a lot of questions that she was scared to seek the answers to. Chanel wondered if James would love her as much as he claimed to now, if she wasn't related to the people who she called "family". Chanel didn't believe that she brought enough to the table for James to appreciate her and look at her with that same glimmer that everyone looked at Farren with. Even though James broke his neck to make sure she was straight, Chanel cried in the tub. She wished it easy to gain confidence. She wanted to wake up in the morning feeling like the prettiest girl in the world, but in reality that's not how she felt. She was an insecure, single mom who was a recovering drug addict and couldn't leave her abusive boyfriend.

It wasn't as if Q's dick was just mind-blowing good, because she didn't have a problem in that department; James made love to her on the daily. Chanel's mind or heart wasn't even in the bed or between the sheets when Q stroked her pussy, her mind was on her life. She knew she was tiptoeing with the devil, but the thrill of Q caused her to spread her pussy lips further and flip over on all fours. Chanel couldn't leave him if she wanted to, it was her mind that he had wrapped around his finger and as bad as she wanted to admit that she deserved better, Q was on her level. They came from the same struggle and tax bracket. Q wouldn't expect her to wear heels on every single date, Q wouldn't ask her to take vitamins every morning and run three fucking miles, Q was unconcerned with prayers and burning sage in the house to keep negativity from the door step.

But the immaturity in Chanel held her back; it was as if she had a pair of strong hands over her eyes to keep from seeing better for herself. If Chanel didn't want more for herself, nobody else could want it for her. What Chanel failed to realize was that she held the power to be better, to become the woman she desired to be. The difference between Chanel and Farren is that Farren never looked up to anyone. She didn't have a role model, nobody inspired her...none of that shit. Farren had always wanted to be Farren.

Chanel needed to get her own heart, her own mind, her own goals and aspirations. She cried in the cold bath water for hours because she was seriously soul-searching and had continually come up empty handed. She didn't know what she was looking for or expecting out of life.

The next morning, Chanel stared at her alarm going off, debating if she was really about to keep working out. Half of her wanted to go because she knew she couldn't keep letting her sister down and not sticking to her word, and the other half of her was like "fuck everybody, "I'm tired and my pussy still hurt".

Chanel didn't know what to do, but she did know that she was sleepy as hell. She turned her cell phone off, and rolled over and went back to sleep.

Farren knew she wasn't coming, she didn't even bother wasting her time getting out of bed, leaving the comfort of her home and her children to chase down a grown ass woman...but James did. Poor James...he had so much faith in his dear Chanel. He twirled the ring around his finger and put it back his glove department, and locked it back before putting his car into reverse and leaving the park. James had never been dismissed by a woman in his life. He didn't even let women get this close to him, but somehow Chanel crept through the steel gates that protected his heart. He didn't want to give up on his sweet lady, but James had never in his life chased pussy or played the fool. He was a very intelligent man and didn't believe in beating a dead horse. Chanel didn't have long to make her mind up about what she was looking for and who she wanted to be with, before James would wipe his hands of her ass.

A few days later, Farren had to pick Madison up because apparently Chanel had forgotten to pick up her daughter. Farren didn't mind picking up her precious daughter, but the issue with Farren was what if there was no auntie Farren listed as the emergency contact, who would be picking Madison up from summer camp.

Farren didn't understand how a bitch could leave her child basically stranded. Farren didn't give a damn what she went through on a daily basis or what problems her and Christian were facing, she never ever let that interfere with how she interacted with and raised her children. A mother's job was never ever done and Chanel had a lot to learn. There was no more "Big Mama". Chanel had to step it up because in all honesty, Farren had her own damn bad ass kids to raise, she didn't have time to see about nobody else kids. If Farren could raise three traumatized kids at that, then the least she could do is see about the one baby God blessed her with.

Farren continued on with her day with the children; she wouldn't let Chanel's dumb ass piss her off. Her and the children spent a beautiful day out in the A, but once night fell, Farren made her way to Chanel's house. According to her daughter, Daddy had been staying there since Monday.

Farren knocked on the door a few times, before using the key Chanel had given her sister when she was living there for a few weeks.

Farren told Madison to hold on before coming into the house. She didn't know what kind of scenario Chanel's daughter would be walking into.

Farren walked around the house, not seeing any visible signs of Chanel. She took the steps upstairs and the door to the master bedroom was wide open. Chanel and the sorry nigga Q was buried under the covers. Farren had to cover her nose with the collar of her Burberry polo shirt. The room reeked of pussy and alcohol and it smelled like feet and onions. Farren almost threw up in her mouth.

Farren cleared her throat and they apparently were so intoxicated, nobody heard her. Farren used an umbrella that was on the floor and used the hook of the umbrella to pull the cover off Chanel, who was still unfazed by any movement or noise.

Farren wanted to grab the dumb bitch by her hair but she decided not to touch her. Farren assumed that her little sister probably hadn't bathed in a few days. Farren shouted, "Chanel Cavett!" Chanel stirred in her sleep, thinking she was in a dream until she rolled over and saw her sister glaring at her.

"Farren?" she said.

"Get your ass up, your daughter is downstairs," Farren told her.

Q was snoring so loud it was ridiculous.

Chanel pulled the comforter over her naked body.

"I will meet you downstairs," she told her sister.

Farren huffed and stepped back over piles of dirty clothes and went back to the foyer area. She told Madison to go get some clothes for the next days because she would be spending the night with Morgan and Noel for the rest of the week.

"Thank you for dropping her off, I overslept. I've been taking them muscle relaxers for my shoulders," she said.

Farren rolled her eyes, "what is wrong with you? You need to get it together and you should never, ever greet guests with un-brushed teeth, that is so not lady like," Farren complained.

Chanel didn't feel like hearing her sister's mouth, she just fucking didn't.

"Okayyyy, thank you, goodbye," she spat.

"You don't dismiss me, I'm the only family you got and I'm trying to help you."

Chanel crossed her arms, "Help me how? You don't care about me, you just want to know why I haven't been coming to practice and I got a deal for you, you can take it or leave it."

Farren laughed, "I can't wait to hear this."

"I'm not going to the Roundtable if Q can't get a seat," she said sassily.

Farren stood. "Madison, you ready baby? Auntie will be in the car."

"Did you not hear me?" Chanel asked.

"No I did not because you not talking about shit," Farren told her straight up.

"My daughter will be staying here, we don't need you," Q said from the top of the steps.

Chanel went to the steps. "Quincy, please go back up the steps."

Farren walked behind her, "Yes Quincy please go back up the steps," she said in her perfect Stepford wife tone.

"Farren I got this okay," Chanel said.

"I can't tell boo boo," Farren said, touching a bruise that had formed under her lip and it was an ugly bruise too.

"Let me go!" Farren smiled. Chanel thanked her again for dropping Madison off.

Farren turned around and imitated a gun motion at Q. He blew her a kiss back and Farren couldn't do anything but smile.

Chanel slammed the door in Farren's face and went to tend to her daughter. Farren had to be more respectful or she wouldn't be allowed over her house anymore.

Farren shook her head once she returned to the car. Her children were knocked out. That Atlanta heat had drained the hell out of them. Her sister was an idiot, and it was nothing that she could do about it. Farren's body was hurting and all of the walking she did today didn't make it any better. Farren called her sister while she drove home. "I need you to come here for a few days," Farren said.

"I can't sis; I'm getting ready for a health inspection, why, what's wrong?" Neeki asked.

"I think I need surgery and I just need some help around the house until I'm completely healed," she said.

"Where is Chanel and Farren, your ass been needing surgery," she got on her sister's ass.

"Well bitch I'm handling that this week, I can't keep being in pain and I'm trying to leave them pain killers alone, and girl, she got too much going on honey, I ain't got time," Farren said.

"Hmmm, well I'll try to come but no promises."

"No worries, my kids can see about themselves honestly, and I'll see if Kennedy can come spend the night, I got enough room," she said.

"Girl, where that nigga Kool at, that's what he's for?"

"He's bipolar," Farren said rolling her eyes. Kool was too up and down for her. She wasn't chasing after no nigga, period.

"Okay, well my boo just got out the shower, I will call you tomorrow," Neeki said hanging up, not even waiting on a response from her big sister.

Farren felt her soul aching but she knew that she had to keep her head up. She couldn't allow anything to get her down or unfocused right now. At times like this, Farren wished she was married, had a husband to wait on her hand and foot, and nurse her back to good health. Farren missed her best friend, Ashley who was the world's best godmother. Ashley would have been over to Farren's house in a heartbeat, and even Farren's mom. Although she didn't really like kids, if Farren really needed her help, she would have been on the first flight to Atlanta, Georgia.

Farren leaned her head on the window and quickly wiped a tear that wanted to fall down her face.

She told herself, "No tears Farren, no tears." She constantly had to keep herself encouraged because if not, she would break at any second.

Chapter 11

"Are you sure you're going to be okay?" Kool asked her.

Farren smiled and nodded her head. "Yes, I promise, you been here forever!" she teased.

"Shawty, don't act like you want me out of here," he said, seriously.

"And if I do?" she asked.

Kool's lip curled up; she knew he was getting mad. He was such a sweetie when he wanted to be, but for the most part, he got on her fucking nerves. But for the past few days, he had been everything she needed him to be, a nurse, cook, caregiver, taxi for the kids. But the streets of Charlotte was calling and Kool had to go handle something for two days.

"So does your niece know I'm dropping the kids off?" he asked, for the millionth time.

"Yes, why you keep asking me that?" Farren asking, picking up on his uneasiness.

Kool ran his hands over his waves, "Mannnnn," he said.

Farren mocked him, "Mannnnnn, what?"

"I used to fuck lil' shawty back in the day," he admitted.

Farren wanted to choke on her water but couldn't.

"Oh my," she mumbled.

"When? Was this recently?" she asked.

He stood. "Nah, nah, when she was going to Spelman, this was years ago, but she only called me when she wanted some money," he told her.

Farren didn't know how to feel. "I'll have my sister drop them off, don't worry about it," Farren said.

"So now you mad? At least I told the truth," he said.

"Just go," she told him.

"Farren...baby," he pleaded.

"Kool, for real, I'm good, just tired," Farren told him and that wasn't a lie. She needed rest. Although her surgeries weren't life-threatening procedures, no one was comfortable with more than a hundred stitches keeping their body together.

"I love you, you know that," he told her.

Farren rolled her eyes. Niggas loved to throw the "I love you" in there when the girl was mad. Farren knew that the situation with him and Kennedy was before her, but still, it made her feel old as fuck. Kennedy was she and Christian's LITTLE niece, literally. She used to let Kennedy ride with her before she had children of her own. Farren had to leave these young niggas alone.

"I feel like your sugar mama," she complained.

"You the sexiest mama I ever had," he laughed and kissed her all over her face.

Farren giggled, "Move...I'm sore," she told him.

"I'll be back before you know it bae, for real," he told her.

Farren rolled her eyes. "Let me call my crackhead sister," Farren said.

"Don't say that," he warned her.

"No I'm serious, she's a crackhead," Farren said with big eyes.

Kool shook his head. He knew Farren was being sarcastic. Chanel didn't look the same but he didn't think she was back on drugs.

"I'll tell Mike to lock up," Kool told her, picking up his duffel bag.

Farren scrolled through her iPhone looking for her sister's number, since she had taken her out of her favorites.

"Hello," Chanel mumbled.

"Are you sleeping?" Farren asked.

"Is this my sister?" Chanel asked yawning.

"Yes it is, Farren Knight," Farren said cheerfully. Surgery and all, nothing could keep Farren Knight down. She had been ordering furniture to finish the other rooms in her house, and even talking to a non-profit organization about working there three days out of the week.

"I need a favor, if Quincy will let you leave the house," she said.

"Farren chill out, what's up?" Chanel asked.

"Can you come get my kids and take them to their auntie Kennedy house? They're going to stay there until Kool gets back," she said.

"What's wrong?" Chanel actually sounded concerned.

"I had surgery the other day," Farren told her. What she wanted to say was if you wasn't so stuck up under that sorry ass nigga you would have known that.

"You good?" she asked.

"Yeah, just don't want the kids to be stuck in the house or getting on my nerves," Farren said honestly.

"And how are you going to eat and stuff?" Chanel asked.

Farren chewed on the top of her pen, "I haven't thought about that, I will figure it out," she said.

"Why haven't you been called me?" Chanel said. She was already climbing out of bed and preparing things for a shower.

"You've been busy honey, you know I don't like to be a bother," Farren said.

"Mmm hmm, I will be there soon," Chanel said.

"Thanks boo boo," Farren said and ended the call.

Thump.

She thought she heard something since her bedroom window was positioned where she could hear everything by the front door, but she chalked it up as her being delusional.

"Mommy, can I come in here with you?" Noel peeped her head in the door.

"Of course boo, come on, mommy was just about to book us a vacation, where would you like to go?" Farren asked.

"Ooooh, Disney World," she said.

"Umm, no. No heat and no walking. What about Barbados?" Farren asked.

"Where is that?" Noel asked.

"It's pretty, lots of sand and tequila for mommy," Farren said.

"I just want to get a massage," Noel said, laying her head on her mom's pillow.

"A massage? Chile, you don't do nothing all day but eat, play, and shit," Farren laughed.

"My back be hurting," Noel complained.

"Girl, please." Farren couldn't take Noel serious, but her daughter was telling the truth.

They spent the next twenty minutes looking at different hotels and resorts.

"Awww, look at y'all," a voice said.

Farren couldn't believe she had finally got caught slipping for real.

"Now Farren don't look like that, the kids are not dead... sleeping with a little help of some special medicine, but not dead," Mario said.

Farren started hyperventilating. It didn't make it any better when Noel climbed into her mother's lap and whispered, "I am scared."

"Mario, let me put my child in the closet," Farren said. She knew that she had no strength to stand but in a matter of life of death, she didn't give a damn. She couldn't believe she didn't have her gun in the bed with her.

"No, I won't be here long. She can stay right where she is. My aim is pretty good, hopefully I don't miss your head," Mario pointed the gun in her direction.

Farren wanted to fucking kill herself she was so damn pissed.

"Let me tell you how God works in mysterious ways, that's what you used to say in Dubai right?" he teased.

Farren clenched her jaw, but Mario continued.

"I was just going to shoot the house up and all of that, but when I saw your little boy toy coming out of the house, I said LOOK AT GOD!" Mario started praise dancing around Farren's room. He was so high it was ridiculous.

"So anyway, I shot his ass up and walked right in the house."

"Mario, what do you want?" Farren asked.

"Well if you would have asked me that a few months ago I would have said YOU, FARREN. I WANT YOU! But of course that's over with," he told her.

"Your mother knew I loved you too, she used to tease me about it when I was younger," he told her.

Farren shook her head, "What?"

"Farren shut the fuck up. You love to act like you don't know shit, I bet you didn't know Christian killed my sister either, did you?" he said.

"Mario..." Farren called his name.

"Your perfect husband...he knew I looked up to him, he knew I loved him and my dad loved him, but he was fucking my little sister and didn't even care. He was so cocky about it. Christian would smile right in the camera cus he knew I was watching," Mario said, wiping his tears with the butt of the gun.

Farren held her daughter's ears in her hands; she wanted her child to have happy memories about her father.

"Where was I? Okay, so yes, your mother knew and she knew what happened to Carren was all Christian's fault."

"Come on now, you know Dice's brother didn't have any connection with anyone in The Cartel. Think Farren, think, did your dumb ass husband ever have an explanation for what REALLY happened to Carren...a daughter for a daughter. Christian killed my sister because she threatened to get him kicked out of The Cartel if he didn't leave you. My sister was losing her mind, she shot at your truck that night...I was in the car with her begging her not to mess with you...loving you from afar but you never ever noticed me," he said sadly.

"What is all of this?" Farren finally let tears come down her eyes.

Farren thought to herself, *How much more damage was this man going to do to me? Even from his grave I'm still being affected by his bullshit.*

Mario told her, "I tried my hardest to love you, but you're just like your husband. Sneaky, conniving, evil, all you do is fucking lie," he shouted at Farren, coming near her.

Noel held her mother's waist tight; Farren's chest was so wet from her daughter's tears and sobs.

"All those nights I sucked your pussy dry, only for you to tell me you was tired when I was ready to fuck, you think I'm a fool Farren?" he shouted.

Mario put the gun to her head and Farren's mind went back to the first night she ever met Christian Knight...that's when she knew then and there at the Waffle House, the motherfucker had been lying from the beginning.

"So you are single or you're not?" Farren asked Mr. Christian Knight.

"What's your definition of being single? Nah, I'm lying...I'm single. Very single," he told her.

"But you are having sex with women right?" she asked.

"Why does that matter if I am here with you at three in the morning?" he flashed a beautiful smile.

"You're full of shit," she laughed. Farren knew she had to be careful with this character; he was entirely too smooth for her, and if she didn't keep her head on her shoulder, she knew Christian Knight could easily have her mind gone.

Farren snapped back into reality, tears ran down her face. She couldn't believe that the majority of the bullshit she had gone through in the past two years, came from her dealings with Christian Knight. It pained her to know that this man...this man whom she loved with every single fiber in her body, had hurt her to the core, destroyed her, ruined her, erupted her existence, cleared her sanity and dragged her through hell and back, oh, and back again.

Farren gave it all up to be with Christian Knight; not physically but mentally, emotionally, spiritually. She knew that being with him wasn't safe...she knew that becoming his wife wouldn't be easy. The perks of being The Connect's Wife is not why Farren married Christian Knight, let's be completely clear. She married him because he was the light of her soul, the joy of her Sunday mornings, and the sun on a gloomy day. She really couldn't imagine life without her better half. But the hurt, the lies, infidelity, abuse, and embarrassment had turned her into a scorned woman. She was bitter and evil. Farren saw her wedding flash before her eyes, the suicide attempt, abortion, miscarriages, the only two visits he received from her, the birth of her beautiful children...Farren wondered had it all really been worth it?

What would her life had been like if she wasn't The Connect's Wife?

Mario pressed the gun closer to her temple.

"I tried to kill your mother this way, but of course she's way more bitchier than you," he laughed.

Noel screamed, cried, and pouted. Farren pinched her which was to signify be quiet. Farren could only pray that Mario didn't harm her baby. She needed her children to live, to become strong, because only God knows the pain that her children had endured the past few years, dealing with so many losses.

Farren closed her eyes and began to pray. It was as if her soul was praying but her flesh was counting down the seconds until her life was over.

POW!

Farren looked up, she wasn't dead. Noel touched her face. "Mommy," she whispered.

There was no way in the world Farren was still alive. She was starting to feel like she was someone really great and that she had nine lives.

Chanel stood in the doorway; her eyes never left Mario's dead body.

Farren got out of bed and took the gun from her.

"Noel," Farren called her daughter's name.

"Yes mommy," she said, voice shaking and full of tears.

"Close your eyes baby girl and cover your ears," she said, voice full of venom.

Farren stood over Mario's body and let the bullets go. She had to make sure this motherfucker had no chance of living and the last bullet was for her mother, may her soul rest in peace.

Chanel threw up right on her sister's bedroom floor.

"Let me call James," Farren mumbled.

She knew she needed to check on her children but she also needed this body out of her house and the carpet cleaned as soon as possible, because she would be moving. This life, this town, this country was not for her. Farren was getting the hell out of here; there was nothing that could keep her in the United States anymore.

One hour later, James had a crew in and out of the house. Farren's children had sat in a tub full of cold water and once they came to their senses, they screamed from the cold water.

Farren told Noel, "Nothing happened tonight baby, okay? It's not good that your brother and sister know what happened," she said.

Noel understood and she nodded her head and kissed her mother's cheek. Although Farren told her, nothing happened she was still scorned and frightened. Noel wanted to ask her mother who would keep them safe, who was responsible for protecting them, but she didn't want to anger her mother so she just went to bed with tears in her eyes and anger in her heart. Noel was tired of going through this, she wanted her old life back. She missed her sister more than anything in this world.

Farren made a pot of fresh coffee and went to shower. All she could do was thank God for mercy and grace once again; she was forever thankful. Farren hated that Kool had been caught up in her bullshit, but James said that he would be okay.

Farren dried off. She was in a daze; her mind was on so many different situations and she just wanted to go spit on Christian's grave. She was tired of being lied to and played. Farren didn't want to hear any more revelations or secrets; she didn't even care to find out anything else.

She checked on the kids for the millionth time tonight before going downstairs. Chanel was lying down on the couch, while James tipped his crew before closing the door.

"Thank you for everything, you're heaven sent," she told James.

He gave her a tight hug, "Anytime," he told her.

"I can't believe she killed him," Farren whispered, assuming that Chanel was knocked out.

"From the looks of where the bullets hit, it might be safe to say that she shoots better than you," James said. He didn't know Farren finished the job and honestly, Farren didn't give a damn where the bullets landed. His heart had shut down and eyes were stuck that was all that mattered to her.

Chanel snatched up her keys and headed to the foyer.

"Sis you saved my life... thank you so much," Farren said. She felt herself getting emotional but knew that there were no more tears left in her.

Comment [RBES]: Sentence is incomplete.

"You're welcome, I need a favor," she said quickly.

James just knew this girl wasn't about to ask for a financial payment for saving her sister's life.

Farren ears perked up, she couldn't wait to hear this shit.

"Q needs a fair chance at joining the Cartel. Now I do understand there is a protocol, but I would appreciate it if he at least gets a vote," she said.

James yelled, "This is not how this goes, Chanel. He's a nobody. What are his credentials to allow him to even qualify?"

Farren shook her head, "Are you serious?"

Chanel nodded, "It's not personal, this is business."

Farren yelled, "You are one stupid bitch."

Chanel got in her face. That one little murder had her feeling herself. "I'm that one stupid bitch that just saved your kids from becoming orphans," she said and walked out of the house.

Farren really couldn't believe her sister. That dude, Q really had her mind messed up to the point where Farren wanted to get custody of Madison. Chanel wasn't even the same loving, sweet, growing young woman. She had damn near fell off the face of the earth. Farren knew she couldn't really point the finger. She had been stupid for Christian and even a few others back in her ratchet days, but never ever had she allowed a nigga to beat her ass. There was never any excuses to be made for a man who found it acceptable to bring hurt and harm, and sometimes even danger to his lady.

Women were to be honored, cherished, and appreciated. Not hurt and disrespected. It was ungodly to be so ugly and rude. What Farren wanted for Chanel was true happiness and love; she wanted Chanel to know that she had a good ass nigga right before her, who was just waiting on her to grow up. Farren found it weird that Chanel would even run back to Q's arms, the same pussy ass nigga that dipped on her once The Cartel came knocking on her door. Weak links were always deleted first. Farren couldn't force Chanel to realize what she was missing out on; experience had to be her teacher.

She just prayed that

The old Farren would have snatched her by the head, but the new at peace, angelic Farren couldn't do anything but go fix her a cup of coffee. James joined her at the breakfast table.

"He was not a part of the plan," Farren said.

James agreed.

"And how do you plan on handling this?" he asked.

Farren sat her coffee mug on the table. "Do you love her?" she asked.

Without much thought or hesitation, James said, "Yes."

Farren bit her lip, closed her eyes, took a deep breath then said, "Well you need to kill him."

Chapter 12

Farren Knight had been through a lot, that we all could agree on, but the amount of time that was put into chasing down scoundrels and even killing the people that invaded her home, would be a waste of time if Farren didn't attend the Roundtable. They didn't really give her a choice. After several official and unofficial invitations, she knew that she had no choice but to attend the meeting. Farren tossed and turned the night before the meeting; she couldn't sleep. So many nightmares and even her dreams were haunted. Farren didn't know what was going to happen. She was unsure of how her life was about to be after this meeting. Farren didn't even know if she was going to be alive after the meeting. There was a lot of blood on her hands and even a dummy could point the finger at her. She prayed that everything was handled well, but then again, she knew it was going to be some bullshit and she would be well prepared if so.

Kool stared at her as she tossed and turned in her sleep. She had a lot on her mind and for the past few days, Farren had been extremely distant, but he didn't blame her. He, too, had a lot to think about. Farren had been planting thoughts in his head about moving to London and just doing their own thing there, and Kool couldn't lie and say that starting a new life somewhere else didn't sound good right about now. He was over the street life and he had a woman tell him fuck everything else just come enjoy life with her and her children, and Kool thought that shit sounded super good.

"I can't sleep," Farren complained. Her body was covered in sweat. Kool sat up and cut the light on. "Why are you scared to go to the meeting? If that's the case your ass doesn't need to go," he told her.

Farren slid her naked body out of the bed and went into the bathroom to splash her face with some cold water from the sink.

"Now you and I both know that is not possible," she told him, sticking her head out of the door.

"Have you talked to Chanel?" Kool asked.

"Of course not, that stupid hoe gets on my nerves. I want to wring her neck," Farren cringed.

She really hated how weak and vulnerable her sister was. A nigga has never had that much control over Farren. Even when she was a youngin' dating older men, Farren had them running circles around her ass. Farren was constantly telling her sister, "A man is to wait on you and work for your time." It was as if she didn't understand it or didn't care to comprehend. Farren wished Chanel would open her eyes and see her worth; she had so much to offer HERSELF, not a man, but HERSELF. Chanel could be so much further in life than she was, but she was forever putting herself on the back burner. Farren had never seen a bitch move so fast when a man called. Farren would leave them waiting by the phone for days before she returned a call. Respect had to be earned, lingerie and heels had to be earned, cum being swallowed definitely had to be earned, steak and potatoes for dinner and breakfast served in bed had to be earned. If you pull out the fireworks during the first three months of the relationship, what does a man have to look forward to? Nothing at all.

Farren's mother may have been a lot of things, mean, rude, secretive, angry, and bitter, but she had never been a dummy. Nakia would tell both of her daughters, "y'all have diamonds in between your legs so act like it."

Kool called out to his girl, "Baby come back to bed."

Farren stared at herself in the mirror. The bags under her eyes from lack of sleep and a little hint of depression and anxiety, showed signs of giving up. Farren had no problem admitting that she was extremely tired. She just wanted to retire somewhere on the beach drinking peach mojitos, watching her children grow old. Farren had already purchased a townhouse in London and hired a staff; they were just waiting on her arrival.

Farren loved life. She had always enjoyed the finer things in life, but she realized one day that none of that mattered. It didn't mean anything to her because it didn't bring her real peace or happiness. Farren would do anything to have her loved ones here with her today. She missed her best friend, she missed her every single day that she breathed air. Ashley was her everything and in this lifetime, it was hard to find females that loved you and wanted the best for you, that cared and prayed for you. Farren would never find someone as genuine as Ashley ever again.

Farren missed Christian Knight, not even because of the bomb ass sex or the memories that they created, but because her children were growing up without their father. Farren missed him because he made her the bad bitch that she knew she was. Farren missed his wisdom and the power that oozed out of his pores. She missed his jokes, his business advice...she missed his swag. Farren had fell in love after Christian Knight true enough, but Christian Knight's love was a love that could never be categorized or described.

Farren missed Jonte, because he loved her hard and he loved her children even harder. Farren wouldn't have been able to grow in the Cartel if it wasn't for Jonte. Jonte was her eyes and ears in the streets; she loved how protective he was of her. Jonte lived, ate, and slept Farren. He considered being with her a blessing and he died proving his love to her. Farren hate it took so much stupid shit to transpire between them before they both realized that they loved each other and no one else was for them. Farren would forever love him because he gave her Morgan.

Farren took her time wiping her tears before she took a deep breath and took a Benadryl. She needed sleep. It was three in the morning and in a few hours, she would be boarding a private flight to fly her to Miami, Florida, for the last Roundtable meeting she planned on attending. Farren was putting this life behind her. It was other shit she wanted to do with her life, and hanging with professional drug dealers and killers wasn't on her to-do list.

On the other side of town, James Morgan was sitting in a rental, humming to his favorite Marvin Gaye song; he smoked on a blunt and sipping on coconut water. James hated wearing all-black; he was a natural kind of man. James had stopped eating meat and was working out three times a day instead of one. He had started getting lazy dealing with all of Farren's bullshit, but after this last kill, he was done with anything associated with the Cartel. James left that life many years ago and would be damned if he ended up in a prison cell for those fuckers. James had to handle this one last situation only because it was personal. James wasn't an emotional man, he didn't even speak that much, so when he did, he expected people to take him serious. James used his actions to express how he felt...and his heart had Chanel Cavett written all over it, but Chanel was blindsided by that sorry cocksucker, Quincy.

James always thought Farren was a little looney, but the best advice she could have ever given him was to kill Q, and that's what he was about to do. James didn't want to be without Chanel. Everything about her screamed his future wife; she just didn't know it yet.

James wasn't all the way right in the head. After he made sure his gun wasn't on safety, he opened his middle console and pulled out the black velvet box that held the engagement ring. James asked himself, "Do I kill his ass then propose? Or let him watch me take his bitch?"

James started to call Farren but decided against it. He put the box in his front pocket. James kept his front door unlocked and the car running. He had been trained by the best murderers in the business; James could kill someone in less than thirty seconds. He didn't plan on being in Chanel's house long, but then again, he had to propose. James tossed his head back and forth trying to decide how he was about to do this.

He nodded at his cleanup crew posted up in the Comcast van on standby. As soon as they saw James exit the house, they knew to enter round the back, clean the house, and dispose of the body. These little fuckers had been making a lot of money in the past few months, strictly off Farren's trigger finger.

James used his key to enter Chanel's home. He was disappointed to not hear the alarm go off; he told Chanel about that several times. She wouldn't take it serious until some stick-up kids ran up in her house and took her daughter. James hated to be so crucial but that was the life they lived.

James frowned up his nose; the house reeked of trash and a fishy smell. It was sad that the nigga couldn't even take the trash out. It was bad enough he wasn't paying any bills, the least he could do was keep the house clean while Chanel worked all day.

James went to check on Madison, who was sleeping peacefully. He kissed her forehead before taking his hand and sliding it under her nose. He was hoping that she took a deep breath to inhale the sleeping oil.

"What the fuck are you doing?" Chanel asked.

James turned around, shocked that she even heard him come into the house.

James smiled. He wanted to keep a scowl on his face but he was so happy to see her he couldn't help it; Chanel made him so happy.

"James?" Chanel asked again. He didn't see the gun at first but now she wasn't hiding it.

"I see I taught you well," James said.

"Whatever nigga, what are you doing in my house and what was you doing to Maddy?" she asked.

"I came to marry you," he told her.

Chanel laughed, "James, please leave, it's too early in the morning," she told him and turned around.

James came up behind her and grabbed her neck. "This is going to be really quick. Go make me some breakfast so I can propose to you the right way," he told her.

Chanel thought to herself, *why do I always get caught with the psycho niggas?*

"Quincy is here and James, you and I both know I'm not about to just marry you," she said.

"I wasn't giving you a choice boo, now do you want to watch him die or you wanna go cook me some scrambled eggs with cheese and toast? No meat," he told her.

Chanel turned around but James snatched the gun out of her hand before she could even think.

"You was about to shoot at me?" he asked surprised.

"No, but I was going to hit you in the head," she told him.

"What is he doing for you?" he asked.

"You don't understand."

"You damn right I don't," he told her, snatching her up and dragging Chanel to her bedroom.

Chanel tried her hardest to get out of James grasp, but of course she couldn't.

"Chanel, you know I will shoot you in the leg so stop biting me," he threatened her.

Chanel quickly stopped; she knew his ass was not playing with her at all.

James entered the bedroom, gun in one hand, Chanel in the other and still managed to turn the fan off and lights on.

"That's why his ass still sleep." James shook his head at the pipe and other drug related paraphernalia on the nightstand. Chanel was so embarrassed.

She knew she shouldn't be with Q, but she was comfortable. So comfortable that she didn't have the strength to leave. Q would fuck her whether she had red bottoms or new balances on, he didn't care. Q knew Chanel better than she knew herself. But what Chanel failed to realize is that Q didn't want what was best of her, he didn't care about her well-being. If it was up to him, Chanel wouldn't have any of the shit she had now. Quincy had no problem eating out of Chanel's hand or asking for her money. It didn't make him feel less of a man at all.

James wanted so much more for Chanel; he imagined them doing great things together.

Chanel was a dummy, though. She'd rather stay with a man who couldn't do anything for her, in fear of experiencing love with a real nigga.

James sent a shot to the headboard and as he predicted, Q sprang out of the bed.

"What the fuck bra!" he shouted.

Chanel turned her head. Half of her wanted James to kill Q so she could get back on her shit, and half of her wanted to kill James. Chanel really just needed to be alone because she was so lost and confused.

"You gotta go," James stated.

"Chanel man, what the fuck going on?" Q asked. He had already pissed in the sheets.

Chanel had so many silent tears in her eyes. Q had been beating her ass left and right and calling her every name in the book. Quincy was trying to break her self-confidence and make Chanel feel bad for leaving him to rot in jail by himself. She had started to believe the evil things he had begun to say. Q told her that Farren really didn't care about her and a whole bunch of other lies.

Chanel got tired of hearing him scream her name; she grabbed the gun out of James hand and shot his ass up.

Seconds later, his body was riddled with bullets and her bed and walls were plastered with blood. It was crazy because she felt her soul reenter her body; she instantly felt okay.

Chanel looked at James with eyes full of emotion and tears. "Happy now?" she asked, tossing the gun to him and leaving the room.

James was a nigga who always checked everything. He didn't give a damn if the clip was empty or not. Chanel had learned many different shooting techniques, but he still had to make sure the nigga wasn't breathing and had a 0 percent chance of his life being saved.

James checked his heartbeat and there wasn't one. He cracked his neck for good measure.

Chanel was in the kitchen, leaning over the sink crying.

James went over to her. "Are you okay?"

"I just need a few days. I love you, I won't deny that. Just give me a few days," she whispered.

James would give her all the space she needed, as long as her ass knew where home was and that was with him.

He pulled the box out of his pocket, set it on the counter, and kissed her forehead.

"Love you," he told her.

Before he left the kitchen, he told her, "Farren's plane leaves at ten."

James left the house, smiling and doing the money dance; he had his bitch back. Today was the best day of his life.

Farren stepped out of her bathtub. She was doing a lil' dance as she moved around the room. Farren loved her some Mary J. Blige; nobody sung pain like Mary did. Farren needed to check Google to see if Mary had any upcoming concerts. She just wanted to close her eyes and jam to all of her favorite songs.

Farren washed and moisturized her face after brushing her teeth. Noel peeped into her mother's bathroom. "Mommy?" Noel called out to Farren.

"Yes baby?" answered.

"Where are you going?" Noel asked.

"I have to handle some business." Farren moved around her daughter, and put on her diamond earrings, Rolex and Cartier bracelet.

"I want to be like you when I grow up," she said.

"Carren...I mean Noel, sorry baby. No, you want to be better than me, way better than me," she told her daughter.

"You're my role model," Noel added.

Farren felt defeated. Ever since Noel was in the room when Mario was killed, she had been clinging to her like crazy, asking creepy questions and saying she wanted to be a ninja. If Farren didn't regret anything else in life right about now, Farren wished she would have removed her daughter from that scene before the shooting.

"Noel, go watch a movie with your sister, let mommy get dressed," Farren told her. Farren had a lot on her mind and needed to smoke before she headed to Miami. Farren let the Ralph Lauren terry towel fall to the floor and she walked into her closet that was really big enough to be another master bedroom in her home. Farren put on a nude thong and half bra.

She sat on the chaise in her closet and laid back, inhaling on some good weed. Farren had everything she needed. Her accounts were full of commas and she had recently purchased a few investment properties. Farren was all about tripling the value of a dollar and spent ample amounts of time researching ways to flip old money. Kool came into her closet. "The movers are here," he told her.

"Perfect," she said, exhaling.

"You good?" he asked her.

"Yes."

"So, I'll meet you there?" Kool told her.

"Sounds good to me," Farren told him with a smile.

She had made her mind up and London was where she really wanted to be. Farren had made so many beautiful memories in the country and was looking forward to making even more. Kool was cool and his sex was good, so if Farren didn't have any other reason to bring him along, it was to get some good dick and toe-curling head on the regular. She had enough money to support his lifestyle and hers and Kool told her he wanted to open a gentlemen's club over there in the next few months. Farren was all for it. She learned to stop letting monetary things define her happiness and Kool really did make her happy.

Farren got up and slid into a white pencil skirt and a white button down shirt. She stepped her feet into a pair of black Prada python pumps. She decided to do her makeup on the plane but she didn't plan on doing much but adding a fresh coat of red lipstick to her lips and eyeliner.

Farren kissed her kids and told her sister, "Don't let them run you crazy," she said. Neeki was rolling with Kool to London and she would meet them there.

Farren had found the perfect home and she had two things on her to-do list before she left: visit Carren and Christian's gravesite, and travel to Miami.

Farren thanked the driver for opening the door to the rental and she sat in the back seat, with her shades on her face.

Farren hummed her wedding song; she made a big step by taking her wedding ring off and throwing it down the sewer on a local street when she was going to get her nails done. Farren had plans of giving the ring to Michael when it came time for him to marry, but after finding out more and more bullshit about Christian's trifling ass, she considered it disrespectful to even pass that ring down. She felt like the ring was a curse and she wouldn't dare put those roots or evil spirits on her son's union.

The car came to a complete stop and Farren took her time walking through the grass. She had fresh roses in her hand from her garden. Farren kneeled in front of her daughter's grave. "Hey kiddo," she said with a smile.

The loss of her daughter was pain on another level and she could never, ever describe it.

"We're moving to London, but I promise you we will be here every year on your birthday, you know Noel wouldn't have it any other way," she said.

Farren took a deep breath. "I love you baby girl." Farren touched the concrete with her daughter's name engraved on the site and her birthday only. Farren didn't believe in celebrating death, so she didn't have the day Carren was killed on there.

Farren kissed the grave and walked over to Christian's.

"I'm going to handle this one last thing for you then that's it," she said in a harsh tone. Farren didn't know why she was always so emotional when she dealt with or thought about Christian Knight.

"I hate you so fucking much," she said, wiping tears from her eyes.

Anyone who saw Farren would think that she was a weirdo talking to a grave, but she continued.

"I loved you but you shitted on me for years; even from your grave you're still haunting me."

Farren looked at her watch, she had to go. The Cartel was really big on time and so was Farren. Business was business and she considered herself a very professional person.

Farren told Christian, "As the Connect's Wife I'm attending this meeting in your honor but this is it for me Chrissy, this shit has brought me nothing but pain."

It was as if she heard his soul telling her to go, so Farren decided to go on and leave the cemetery and the driver had to exceed the speed limit just to get her to the private airport.

Farren ran up the steps, yelling to the pilot, "Let's go."

She didn't even notice her sister. "I thought tardiness was a no-no," Chanel smiled.

Farren was shocked to see her sister. "What are you doing here?"

Chanel wagged her finger. "My FIANCE told me my sister needed me," she teased.

Chanel was happy that she got her act together and quick. After James left her house she went back and forth with her thoughts, fuck with her sister or cut her off. Chanel knew that Farren was the realest on her team so she quickly got some act right, showering quickly and heading over to meet her sister on the plane. Chanel knew that Quincy deserved death; she just prayed that when she closed her eyes to sleep that night that she would be okay.

Instantly, Farren forgot the bullshit her sister said to her the other week. She hopped in her lap and smothered her in kisses.

"Oh my God bitch, you getting married!" Farren was so happy for Chanel and even happier that it was confirmed James handled the job.

The pilot stuck his head in between the velvet curtain. "To Miami correct?" he asked.

Farren looked at her sister. "You sure about this?" she asked.

Chanel nodded.

"I can see myself taking over," Chanel said.

Farren high-fived her little sister and told the pilot let's go.

"Damn, I was married to The Connect, now my sister is The Connect," she said seriously.

"You think they gone vote me in for real?" Chanel asked.

"We will have to see when we get there, but I think so," Farren told her.

Chanel put on her headphones and did some work for The Cavett Agency while Farren looked at furniture online.

The flight attendant handed her a glass of champagne and said, "We will be landing in about twenty minutes.

"I can't believe I'm about to do this shit, give me some advice," Chanel said nervously.

Farren Knight held up her glass and said, "Loyalty is everything."

The Life of Farren Knight

In conclusion of The Connect's Wife, Farren Knight's heart was finally at peace. After burying a host of loved ones she decided that life in the United States was no longer for her. Farren and her children moved to London and began a whole new adventure. Farren was able to experience new foods, religion, and start a plethora of businesses. Anything that Farren touched became successful, but she no longer yearned for money or for power, she just wanted happiness. Farren was a beautiful woman but for many years, how she appeared on the outside wasn't how she felt on the inside. She grew up being known as "that pretty little girl," and now she has transpired into a wonderful young woman. Farren Knight was beautiful, tall, charming, and educated. She was truly a jack-of-all-trades. Farren was flawed but she was also faithful. Without applying much pressure and effort, she forever reigned supreme.

Farren Knight was a woman who went through hell but came out on top every single time. She dominated every situation. Upon traveling to London, a surreal feeling overcame her and she was able to breathe and sleep peacefully at night for the first time since the death of her husband, Christian Knight. Farren was so happy that she didn't have to go from the kitchen to the living room with a gun. Farren's soul was finally at peace. She did everything in life she had ever wanted to. A girl from the slums, she had a successful career, was a pillar in her community, and raised her children to the best of her ability. Farren didn't have any more tears to wipe, she didn't have anything else to complain or worry about. *The life of Farren Knight did a 180 and she was truly one blessed individual.*

Epilogue

One Year Later

"Pass me some of that," Chanel told her husband.

"I hope you don't be shitting on the plane," he told her seriously.

"The joys of having your own shit, I can boo boo all I want," she stuck her tongue out at him, but of course James' nasty ass reached in and started sucking on it.

"Ewww, get a room," Farren teased.

"Honey, I know you not talking, let's not forget why the wedding started late," Neeki snapped on Farren.

"I'm going through menopause," Farren joked. Her and Kool just had to start a quickie ten minutes before Chanel and James' wedding was set to start, and the wedding was thirty minutes behind schedule because Farren just had to catch a nut or two.

"I'm surprised you not sleep," Chanel said.

"Baby, that flight so long to get back to London I'm going to be knocked out tonight," Farren told her sister.

"I hear that," James agreed.

One of Chanel's security guards came and whispered in her ear. James instantly became irritated. It was their wedding night, not a night to discuss business, especially with the stupid Cartel. James knew that Chanel wouldn't hesitate to get up and see what was going on because that's just how she had become over the past year. But she promised the night before when she was riding his dick that tomorrow was all about them. Chanel just wanted to spend quality time with her sister before she returned back to her new country.

"I will be right back y'all," Chanel said, holding up her wedding dress as she slid out of the decorated chair.

Chanel nor Farren held back when it came to her wedding. Chanel broke the bank for her wedding because she told herself this was her first and last wedding. Farren was tempted to get married again just because her sister's wedding was so lavish, but Kool told her they didn't need none of that, so Farren just put her all into making Chanel's wedding a day she would never forget. Farren got up from the seat. "I wanna come, I haven't sat in on a meeting in forever," Farren said seriously.

Neeki shouted, "Girl, sit your wanna be gangster ass down."

Farren flipped her the middle finger and followed her sister.

Kool shook his head right along with James. One thing about those sisters, they didn't play about their business.

Chanel and Farren walked to one of the storage rooms in the building where Chanel's reception was being held.

Everyone made way for Chanel once she walked in the room. Farren was impressed to see the amount of respect the families and new members of the Cartel had showed her. Chanel had put her time in and she deserved the position as head of the Cartel. Last year at the Roundtable she was voted in but had to wait a year for her thoughts to be heard, and when they did hear them she was instantly promoted. Sure enough, a few people had some choice words, but Chanel proved to them, and even herself that she was well qualified to run the position.

"What's going on?" Chanel got straight to the point.

"I think there was a FED here," one of the members spoke up.

Farren's heartbeat sped up...the FEDS were like a disease amongst the Cartel.

Noel came into the room. "Ma," she said.

Farren looked over a few of the taller people that were in her way. "Is that my kid?" she asked.

"Noel, what are you doing in here?" Farren asked.

"I know what y'all meeting about, can I please stay, I want to help?" she pleaded.

Farren was shocked to hear her little child say that. Although Noel was growing up, she damn sure wasn't GROWN.

"Girl if you don't carry your ass on," Farren snapped.

Noel pouted but she did obey her mother and closed the storage door.

"We have a little Christian Knight on our hands," one of the older members spoke up.

Farren shook her head, "Like hell."

Chanel made eye contact with her sister. "I told you...you gotta watch that one," she said.

Farren thought to herself *I hope not.*

"Who was the federal agent?" Chanel got back to business.

"I'm not sure," the man said.

"Well how are you even sure?"

"I just know...trust me," he said.

Chanel shook her head. This was not what she wanted to deal with or think about. She was set to travel to a private island tonight with her husband.

Chanel waited until everyone left the room and it was just Farren and her remaining in the room.

"What do I have to do?" Chanel asked.

Farren hummed as she went into deep thought. "Hmm..."

"Man come on," she told her, ready to do the electric slide with her people.

"Turn up," Farren said.

Chanel was confused, "And what the fuck does that mean?"

Farren said, "Takeover the Cartel. Shut it down and start over."

The Connect's Wife 7 Is Now On Amazon

To stay updated with upcoming releases like Nako's author page. www.Facebook./Nako

Instagram: nakoexpo

If you enjoyed the story, please leave a **review**!

Authors love REVIEWS!

For more updates and sneak peeks into **upcoming** releases written by NAKO

Text NAKOEXPO to 22828

www.facebook.com/NAKO

Twitter: nakoexpo

Instagram:nakoexpo

Snapchat: penprissy

Join **NAKO'S READING GROUP** on Facebook…we're more than a reading group, join today and find out!

Join **NAKO'S READING GROUP** on Instagram…we're more than a reading group, join today and find out.

Join **@ALLTHINGSNAKO** on Twitter, we're more than a reading group, join today and find out.

Join **NAKOEXPO** on Facebook to unite with single women who are enjoying life and living it up to the fullest.

Text **SINGLEANDOK to 22828** for more information.

Text NAKOEXPO **to 22828** to join NAKO'S MAILING LIST and exclusive samples on **#samplesunday**

SUBSCRIBE TO NAKO'S YOUTUBE CHANNEL: NAKOEXPO

BEHIND THE PEN IS A BTS LOOK INTO BOOKS WRITTEN BY NAKO!

ALSO, IF YOU'RE INTERESTED IN PURCHASING THE UNDERWORLD VISIT NAKOEXPO.COM OR EMAIL NAKOEXPO@GMAIL.COM TO PURCHASE YOUR COPIES TODAY.

THE FOLLOWING SHIRTS ARE FOR SALE:

"READ PRAY SLAY"

"BOOKS OVER BOYS"

"TRUE LIFE: I'M A BLACK GIRL WITH MAGIC"

"PROUD MEMBER OF NRG"

– VISIT NAKOEXPO.COM OR EMAIL NAKOEXPO@GMAIL.COM TO ORDER TODAY

NAKOEXPO PRESENTS IS NOW ACCEPTING SUBMISSIONS. EMAIL NAKOEXPO@GMAIL.COM FOR MORE INFORMATION OR SEND THE FIRST THREE CHAPTERS OF YOUR MANUSCRIPT FOR CONSIDERATION.

Visit www.nakoexpo.com for **The Passport**, personal stamps written by women for women.

Nako's Catalog

The Connect's Wife 1-7

The Chanel Cavette Story

If We Ruled the World 1 & 2

Love in The Ghetto 1 & 2

The Connect 1 & 2

In Love With A Brooklyn Thug 1-3

The King and Queen of New York

No Fairytales: The Love Story in collaboration with Jessica N. Watkins

The Underworld Series

Please Catch My Soul

Pointe of No Return

From His Rib

The Christ Family

Stranger In My Eyes

Resentment

The Arraignment II

Redemption

Made in the USA
Coppell, TX
09 November 2019

11160492R00097